Delores Fossen, a *USA TODAY* bestselling author, has sold over seventy-five novels, with millions of copies of her books in print worldwide. She's received a Booksellers' Best Award and an RT Reviewers' Choice Best Book Award. She was also a finalist for a prestigious RITA® Award. You can contact the author through her website at www.deloresfossen.com.

Also by Delores Fossen

The Lawmen of McCall Canyon miniseries

Cowboy Above the Law
Finger on the Trigger
Lawman with a Cause
Under the Cowboy's Protection

Blue River Ranch miniseries

Always a Lawman
Gunfire on the Ranch
Lawman from Her Past
Roughshod Justice

The Lawmen of Silver Creek Ranch miniseries

Grayson
Dade
Nate
Kade
Gage
Mason
Josh
Sawyer
Landon
Holden

Discover more at millsandboon.co.uk.

Under the Cowboy's Protection

DELORES FOSSEN

MILLS & BOON

First published in Great Britain 2019
by Mills & Boon, an imprint of HarperCollins*Publishers*
1 London Bridge Street, London, SE1 9GF

Large Print edition 2019

© 2019 Delores Fossen

ISBN: 978-0-263-08378-1

MIX
Paper from
responsible sources
FSC™ C007454

This book is produced from independently certified
FSC™ paper to ensure responsible forest management.
For more information visit www.harpercollins.co.uk/green.

Printed and bound in Great Britain
by CPI Group (UK) Ltd, Croydon, CR0 4YY

Chapter One

Sheriff Raleigh Lawton didn't like the looks of this.

The glass on the front door of the house had been shattered, and the chairs on the porch were toppled over. Both could be signs that maybe there'd been some kind of struggle here.

That kicked up his heart rate a huge notch, and he drew his gun, hoping he didn't need to use it. While he was hoping, he added that maybe there was some explanation for the glass and chairs. Maybe the woman who lived in this small one-story house was okay. Raleigh had a double reason for wishing that.

Because the woman, Sonya Burney, was nine months pregnant.

He'd known her all his life, and that's why Raleigh hadn't hesitated to go check on her when the doctor from the OB clinic had called him to say that Sonya had missed her appointment. In a big city, something like that would have gone practically unnoticed, but in a small ranching town like Durango Ridge, it got noticed all right.

The rain spat at him when he stepped from his truck. It was coming down hard now, with an even heavier downpour in the forecast. He had a raincoat, but he didn't want to take the time to put it on. However, he did keep watch around him as he hurried up the steps and onto the porch.

"Sonya?" he called out and immediately listened for anyone or anything.

Nothing.

He tested the doorknob. Unlocked. And he cursed when he stepped inside. The furniture had been tossed here, too. There was a broken lamp on the floor, and the coffee table was on its side. Raleigh reached for his phone, ready to call one of his deputies for backup, but something caught his eye.

Drops of what appeared to be blood on the floor.

Raleigh had a closer look. Not blood. Judging from the smell, it was paint. And he soon got more proof of that. There was a still-open can in the hall just off the living room, and a discarded brush was next to it. However, it wasn't the can or brush that grabbed his attention. It was what someone had scrawled on the wall.

This is for Sheriff Warren McCall.

Hell.

That felt like a punch to the gut. Because he'd seen a message identical to that one almost a year ago. A message that'd been written in the apartment of a woman who had been murdered. Unlike Sonya, that particular woman had been a stranger to him.

The memories came. Images Raleigh wished that time would have blurred. But they were still crystal clear. The woman. Her limp, lifeless body, and the baby she'd been carrying was missing—it still was.

He prayed that Sonya and the baby wouldn't have similar fates.

Raleigh didn't have any proof of who'd killed that other woman, stolen the child or written that message. But he had always thought the message had been left for him. And Warren, of course.

Warren was his father.

Biologically anyway. Raleigh had never considered the man to be his actual dad. Never would.

He made the call for backup and used his phone to take a quick picture of the message. Actually, it was a threat. Raleigh just hoped that Sonya hadn't gotten caught up in this tangled mess between Warren and him.

"Sonya?" he called out again.

Still nothing, but Raleigh continued to look for her. The house wasn't huge, a combined living and kitchen area, two bedrooms and a bath. He went through each one and didn't see her. But there was another message, and it'd been slopped in red paint on one of the bedroom walls. A repeat of the other one.

The repeat hadn't been necessary. Raleigh had gotten it the first time.

This is for Sheriff Warren McCall.

Warren was retired now, but he'd once indeed been the sheriff of McCall Canyon, a town one county over. He'd also carried on an affair with Raleigh's mom for nearly three and a half decades. Or rather, Warren had *carried on* with her until his secret had come out into the open after someone had tried to kill him. Raleigh's mother had been a suspect in that attack. And Warren's "real" family—his wife, two sons and his daughter—hated Raleigh and her.

Was one of them responsible for this?

Maybe. That was something he would definitely investigate, but first he had to find Sonya.

Since it would take a good twenty minutes for his deputy to get all the way out to Sonya's house, Raleigh kept looking, and he made his way out through the kitchen and to the back porch. The moment he stepped outside, he heard something. At first he thought it was the cool October rain hitting the tin roof.

It wasn't.

There was a woman dressed in jeans and a raincoat. She was facedown, on the end of the porch, and she was moaning. Raleigh ran to her and turned her over, but it wasn't Sonya. However, it was someone he knew.

Deputy Thea Morris.

Seeing her gave his heart rate another jolt. Of course, Thea usually had that effect on him. Not in a good way, either, and it certainly wasn't good now. What the hell was she doing here, and what was wrong with her?

Raleigh didn't see any obvious injuries. Not at first. Then he pushed aside her dark blond hair and saw the two small circular burn marks on her neck. Someone had used a stun gun on her.

"Where's Sonya?" he asked.

Thea opened her eyes, but she was clearly having trouble focusing because she blinked several times. Then she groaned again. She didn't answer him, but he saw the alarm on her face, and she started struggling to sit up. He helped her with that. Too bad it meant putting his arms around her to do that.

And Raleigh immediately got another dose of too-clear memories that he didn't want.

Of Thea being not just in his arms but in his bed. But that was an *old water, old bridge* situation.

"Where's Sonya?" Raleigh repeated. "And what happened to you?" He had other questions, but those were enough of a start, since finding Sonya was his priority right now.

"Sonya," Thea repeated in a mutter. She lifted her hand—not easily because it was practically limp—and she touched her fingers to her head. "Sonya."

"Yeah, that's right. *Sonya.* She's pregnant, and I'm worried about her." *Worried* was an understatement. "What happened to her? What happened to *you*?"

Thea blinked some more, looked up at him, and the concern was obvious in her deep green eyes. "A man. I think he took her."

That got Raleigh's attention, and he fired glances around them, trying to see if he could spot her. But there was still no sign of Sonya.

"The man had a gun," Thea added, and she groaned, trying to get to her feet. She failed and dropped right back down on the porch. She also reached for her own gun, but her shoulder holster was empty. Since she was wearing her badge, Raleigh doubted she'd come here without her gun.

"What man?" Raleigh demanded. "And where did he take her?"

Thea groaned again and shook her head. "I

don't know, but he said he was doing this because of Warren."

Raleigh hadn't actually needed that last bit of info to raise the alarm inside him. With the signs of struggle and those stun gun marks on Thea's neck, he decided it wasn't a good idea for them to be out in the open like this. Sonya's place was an old farmhouse with a barn and a storage shed, but the woods were only a short walk away. It would give an attacker plenty of places to hide.

If the man was indeed hiding, that is. If someone had actually taken Sonya, he could be long gone by now.

"We need to get inside." Raleigh hooked his arm around Thea's waist, pulling her to her feet. She wobbled, landing against him. Specifically against his chest. He shoved aside the next dose of memories that came with that close contact.

"You have to go after the man," Thea said. Her voice was as shaky as the rest of her. "You have to get Sonya."

"I will."

His deputy would be here in ten minutes or so, and Raleigh would start searching as soon as he had someone to watch Thea. She wasn't in any shape to defend herself if her attacker returned. At the moment though, he was much more concerned about Sonya. After all, Thea was alive and okay, for the most part anyway, but Sonya could be in the hands of a kidnapper.

Or a killer.

But that didn't make sense. Who would want to hurt her, and what did any of this have to do with Warren? Unless…

A very unsettling thought came to mind.

"Did this happen because Sonya's a surrogate?" Raleigh asked. He helped Thea into a chair at the kitchen table and then went back to the window to see if he could spot any sign of the woman or the person who'd taken her.

"I don't know. Maybe..." Thea's voice trailed off, and that's when Raleigh noticed that Thea's attention had landed on the painted message on the wall. She shuddered, but she didn't turn away. "I don't suppose you put that there?" But she shook her head, waving off her question. "No. You and Sonya were friends."

Raleigh wasn't sure how Thea knew that, but then he wasn't sure of a lot of things right now. "Start talking. I want to know everything that happened." Though it was hard to stand there and listen to anything Thea had to say when his instincts were screaming for him to go after Sonya.

Thea didn't jump right into that explanation; instead, she got to her feet. "We can talk while we look for her. Do you have a backup gun you can lend me?"

Raleigh frowned. Thea didn't look at all steady on her feet, which meant her aim would probably suck, too. Still, she was a cop.

Warren's star deputy, in fact.

Warren had not only trained her and given Thea her start in law enforcement, his father had made it clear that he loved Thea like a daughter. That was convenient, since Thea loved him like a father.

Raleigh wasn't sure how Thea had managed to overlook the fact that Warren was a lying, cheating snake, and he really didn't care. Heck, at the moment he didn't care if Thea was having trouble standing. She had the right idea about looking for Sonya as they talked, so Raleigh gave her his backup gun from his boot holster.

"I got here about a half hour ago," Thea said,

glancing at the clock on the microwave. While she held on to the kitchen counter, she made her way to the back door. "Sonya didn't answer my call this morning, so I came over to check on her." She paused. "I've been checking on her a lot lately."

"I didn't know Sonya and you were that close," Raleigh commented. Sonya had only moved to Durango Ridge about ten years ago, so it was possible she'd known Thea before then. Or maybe they'd recently become friends. But after one look in Thea's eyes, he knew that wasn't the case.

Raleigh groaned. "This has to do with Sonya being a surrogate."

Thea nodded and managed to get the back door open. "I haven't given up on finding Hannah Neal's killer."

Neither had Raleigh. And he especially wasn't forgetting her now, because that message on Sonya's wall was identical to the one found at Hannah's apartment a year ago. Hannah had been murdered only a couple of hours after she'd given birth. That same person who'd killed Hannah had almost certainly been the one who had taken the newborn.

"Sonya didn't know Hannah," Thea continued, "but they were both surrogates, and they used the same doctor for the in vitro procedures that got them pregnant."

Raleigh's gut twisted. Because he'd known that. And he had dismissed it as being something unimportant. Of course, he sure wasn't dismissing it now.

Still, it didn't make sense. Why would someone go after two surrogates to get back at Warren? Especially since Sonya had no personal connection to Warren.

Or did she?

Raleigh didn't have the answer to that, either, but he soon would.

Thea stepped out onto the back porch, and like Raleigh, she looked around. She also caught on to the porch railing to keep herself from falling. Raleigh nearly had her sit down on the step, but babysitting Thea wasn't his job. His job was to find Sonya.

"Tell me about this man who took Sonya," Raleigh demanded. "Was he here when you arrived?"

Thea nodded and followed him into the yard. Not easily, but she made it while still wobbling and using every last inch of the porch railing. "I saw him. He wore a ski mask and was holding her at gunpoint. He was about six-one and about two hundred pounds."

That tightened his stomach even more. Sonya was barely five-three and had a petite build. She wouldn't have stood a chance against a guy that size. Especially if he had a gun.

Thea stopped once she was in the yard, and with the rain pouring down on her, she looked back at him. "Sonya had the baby. Not with her," she added when she must have seen the shock on his face. "But she was no longer pregnant."

That didn't make sense, either. Sonya's doctor was in town. So was the hospital she'd intended to use to deliver. If she'd had the baby there, Raleigh would have certainly heard about it.

"Did she say anything about the baby? About the man?" Raleigh pressed.

"No. He had her gagged and already in the yard when I got here. I moved toward him, but there must have been a second man. Or a second person. He hit me with a stun gun when I came onto the porch. I think they took Sonya that way." She tipped her head to the woods.

Thea was lucky the guy hadn't killed her. Or maybe luck didn't have anything to do with it. Maybe keeping her alive had been part of the plan.

"I would tell you to wait here, but I doubt you will," Raleigh grumbled to her, and he started for those woods.

He didn't get far though, because he heard the sound of a car engine. At first he thought it might be the deputy, but it was a woman who came running out the back door, and Raleigh recognized the tall brunette.

Yvette O'Hara.

The woman who'd hired Sonya to be a surrogate. Like Thea and him, Yvette was wet from the rain. The woman was breathing through her mouth, her eyes were wide and her forehead was bunched up.

"Where's Sonya?" Yvette blurted out.

"We're not sure." Raleigh figured Yvette wasn't going to like that answer. Judging from her huff, she didn't. But it was the best he could do. "Stay here. Deputy Morris and I were about to look for her."

Yvette glanced at Thea. "What's going on? Did something happen to Sonya, to the baby?" She was right to be concerned—especially if she'd noticed the toppled furniture and messages on the walls.

"Stay put," he warned her again.

But Yvette didn't listen. She barreled down the steps, and also like Thea, she had some trouble staying steady. In her case though, it was because she was wearing high heels.

"Sonya's doctor called me," Yvette said, her words running together. "She missed her appointment. She wouldn't have done that if everything was all right."

Probably not. But Raleigh kept that to himself. Yvette already looked to be in alarm-overload mode, and it was best if he didn't add to that. He didn't want her getting hysterical.

"Just stay here," he said. "That way, if Sonya comes back, she won't be here alone."

Yvette finally gave a shaky nod to that and sank down onto the porch steps. Good. It was bad enough that he had Thea to watch, and he didn't want to have to keep an eye on Yvette, too. If those armed thugs were still in the area, it was too dangerous for Yvette to follow them.

Thea didn't stay back though. Despite her unsteady gait, she kept on walking, straight toward the woods, and Raleigh had to run to catch up with her. He'd just managed that when he heard someone call out to him.

"Raleigh?" It was Deputy Dalton Kane. Since Raleigh hadn't heard a siren, it meant Dalton had done a silent approach, and

Raleigh was glad he was there. He needed some backup right now.

"Stay with Mrs. O'Hara," Raleigh told him. "The woman on the porch," he added in case Dalton didn't know who Yvette was. "And get more backup and some CSIs out here. I want the house processed ASAP."

Again, Thea got ahead of him, and Raleigh had to catch up with her. She didn't even pause when she made it to the trees; she just walked right in. Since it was obvious that she wasn't going to be cautious, Raleigh moved in front of her.

"I think the thugs were parked back here somewhere," Thea said. "Shortly after the one hit me with the stun gun, I believe I heard a vehicle leaving."

Raleigh silently groaned. If that was true, then there was no telling where Sonya could be. "Is it possible one of the men had the baby with him?" he asked.

"No." But Thea paused and shook her head. "Maybe. I didn't get even a glimpse of him. After the stun gun hit, I fell on the porch, and I think I passed out."

Perhaps because she'd hit her head. Raleigh could see the bruise forming on her right cheekbone. Of course, if this was a kidnapping, the person could have even drugged Thea to make sure she didn't come after them.

But who would want to kidnap Sonya?

Raleigh drew a blank. Sonya hadn't been romantically involved with anyone. At least he didn't think she had been, but it was possible she'd met someone. It was something Raleigh hoped he could ask her as soon as they found her.

They kept walking, and it didn't take long for Raleigh to spot the clearing just ahead. He'd been born and raised in Durango Ridge, but he hadn't been in this part of the woods.

However, like the rest of the area, there were paths and old ranch trails like this one that led to the creek.

"The rain is washing away the tracks," Thea mumbled, and she sped up.

She was right—if there were any tracks to be found, that is. And there were. Despite the rain, Raleigh could still see the grooves in the dirt and gravel surface. A vehicle had been here recently. He took out his phone to get photos of the tracks just in case they were gone before the CSI team could arrive. He'd managed to click a few shots when he heard Thea make a loud gasp.

Raleigh snapped in her direction, following her gaze to see what had captured her attention. There, in the bushes, he saw something that he definitely hadn't wanted to see.

Sonya's lifeless body.

Chapter Two

Thea fought the effects of the adrenaline crash. Or rather she tried. But while she was waiting on Sonya's front porch, she was also fighting off the remnants of that stun gun, along with the sickening dread that another woman was dead.

Oh, God. She was dead.

For a few seconds after she'd seen the body, Thea had tried to hold out hope that it wasn't Sonya. That it was some stranger, but that had been an unrealistic hope to have. After all, she'd seen the gunman taking Sonya. She'd known the woman was in extreme danger.

"Why did the gunman even take Sonya from the house?" Thea mumbled. "If he was just going to kill her, why didn't he do that when he first broke in?"

She hadn't intended for anyone to actually hear those questions. Not with all the chaos going on. But Raleigh obviously heard her, since he looked at her. What he didn't do was attempt an answer, because he was standing in the front doorway while giving instructions to the CSIs, who were now processing Sonya's yard and house.

Because it was a crime scene.

One that wasn't in Thea's jurisdiction.

That's why she just sat there on the front porch, waiting for Raleigh to give her some task to do. *Any* task. Anything that would help them find out who'd done this. That wouldn't stop this crushing feeling in her heart though, and it couldn't bring back Sonya. But maybe

Thea could help get justice for the dead woman.

"Please tell me you found the baby," she said when Raleigh finished with the CSIs and started toward her.

He shook his head. "But there's some evidence that Sonya delivered the child here, at her house." Raleigh added a weary sigh to that, and he stopped directly in front of her. "There were some bloody sheets in the washer, and a package of newborn diapers had been opened. So had a case of premade formula bottles. Three of the bottles and four of the diapers were missing."

Well, Sonya had obviously had the baby somewhere, so the delivery could have easily happened here in her home, but that just led Thea to yet another question. Why wouldn't Sonya have gone to the hospital to deliver the child?

However, Thea instantly thought of a bad answer to that.

Maybe the gunman was here when the baby had been born. Those thugs could have stopped her from getting the medical attention she needed.

She looked up at Raleigh, and he was staring at her. His lawman's stare. That meant his comment about the sheets and diapers hadn't been just to catch her up on what they'd found. This was the start of his official interview, since she'd actually seen the man who was likely responsible for murdering Sonya.

Of course, Thea had already told him some details when Raleigh had found her on the back porch, and she had added other bits of info while they'd waited for the CSIs and ME to arrive. Obviously though, he wanted a lot more now.

But Thea didn't have more.

"You should be inside the house with Yvette," Raleigh reminded her. It wasn't the first time he'd mentioned that. "Whoever killed Sonya is still at large, and you could be a target."

"So could you." Best not to mention that the gunmen might want him dead because he was Warren's son.

No.

That would only make matters worse. And as for going inside with Yvette, obviously neither of them wanted to do that, because they both stayed put.

Thea's heart was breaking for Yvette, since the missing baby was her biological child—a daughter, from what Sonya had told her a couple months ago—but Thea didn't have the emotional energy to deal with Yvette just yet. Besides, she didn't even know what to say to the woman. The only thing they could do was hope they found the baby soon, along with finding Sonya's killer.

"I had at least a dozen conversations with Sonya," Thea explained to Raleigh. "I visited her here at her house three times, and not once did she ever hint that she was in any kind of danger."

He made a sound that could have meant anything and kept up the intense stare. He was good at it, too. Unfortunately, looking at him reminded her of other things that had nothing to do with the murder and missing baby.

Once Raleigh had been attracted to her. Obviously not now though. There wasn't a trace of attraction in his stormy blue eyes or on that handsome face. He was all cowboy cop now.

"And you visited Sonya because of Hannah Neal," he said.

It wasn't a question, but Thea nodded to

confirm that. "Hannah was my friend, and it eats away at me that I haven't been able to find her killer."

She caught something in his eyes. A glimmer that she recognized. It ate away at Raleigh, too.

Raleigh hadn't known Hannah, but Hannah's body had been dumped just at the edge of Durango Ridge. That meant it was Raleigh's case, but then, despite his retirement, Sheriff Warren McCall had gotten involved because Hannah had lived in their hometown of McCall Canyon. Plus, Hannah had been murdered in McCall Canyon, too. Murdered, and her killer had left the same obscene message on her wall that he had on Sonya's.

At the time of that investigation, Warren hadn't mentioned a word about Raleigh being his illegitimate son. Neither had Thea, though she had known. She had found out Warren's secret a few months before that, but she hadn't told anyone. And that was the reason she no longer saw the attraction in Raleigh's eyes. He hated her now because she'd kept that from him.

But not nearly as much as she hated herself for doing it.

Thea shook her head to clear it, forcing her mind off Hannah and back onto Sonya. Hannah's case was cold, but what they uncovered here today could maybe help them solve both murders.

"Why exactly did you become friends with Sonya?" Raleigh asked.

It wasn't an easy question. "It didn't start out as friendship. I'd been keeping tabs on the doctor who did the in vitro on Hannah." Actually, she'd kept tabs on anything related to her late friend. "So, when I found out this same doctor, Bryce Sheridan, had done this procedure on another surrogate, I wanted to talk to her. I wanted to see if there were any… irregularities."

Raleigh's eyebrow came up. "You think Dr. Sheridan had something to do with Hannah's murder?"

"No. I mean, I didn't know. I was just trying to find any kind of lead." Thea had to take a deep breath before she could continue. "But after I met and talked to Sonya, I didn't see any obvious red flags. Especially not any red flags about Dr. Sheridan."

That ate away at Thea even more. Because she should have seen something. She should have been able to stop this from happening.

"Both Hannah and Sonya were surrogates," Raleigh said, "and both were connected to you. According to the messages left at the crime scenes, the women were linked to Warren, too."

She couldn't deny that. Thea knew both women and had worked for Warren for three years before he'd retired and turned the reins of the sheriff's office over to his son Egan. It was ironic that all three of Warren's sons had become lawmen, but Thea seriously doubted that Raleigh would ever say that he had followed in his father's footsteps.

"You think I'm the reason these women were killed?" Thea came out and asked him.

Just saying the question aloud robbed her of her breath, and Raleigh didn't even get a chance to answer, because his deputy Dalton came out of the house and onto the porch. He wasn't alone, either. Yvette was with him. The woman was no longer crying, but her eyes were red and swollen, and she had her phone gripped in her hand so hard that her knuckles were white.

"We have to find my daughter, so I hired

some private investigators," Yvette immediately said.

"I told her I didn't think that was a good idea," Dalton mumbled.

It wasn't. PIs, even well-meaning ones, could interfere with an investigation to the point of slowing it down, but Thea couldn't fault Yvette for doing this. The woman had to be desperate because her baby could be in the hands of a killer.

"You saw Sonya," Yvette said to Thea. "How was she? Was she weak? Did she say anything about the baby?"

Yvette had already asked these questions several times and in a couple of different ways. So had Raleigh. But Thea didn't mind answering them again. Maybe if she kept going over what she'd seen, she would remember something else. It was a tactic that cops used to try to get more info from witnesses.

"Yes, she looked weak," Thea admitted. "And scared. The man who took her had his arm around her waist as if holding her up."

Even though that wasn't new information, it caused fresh tears to spring to Yvette's eyes. "What about the second man, the one who had the stun gun. Is it possible he had the baby with him?"

Thea had already considered that and had mentally walked through every moment of the attack. "It's possible. I didn't even see him. In fact, as I said earlier, it could have been a woman."

Yes, she had indeed said that earlier, but this time it caused Raleigh to shift his attention to Yvette. And Yvette noticed the abrupt shift, too.

"Well, it wasn't me," Yvette snapped. "I'd have no reason to take my own child and murder the woman who carried her for nine months."

No obvious reason anyway, but it was odd that the woman had assumed they were thinking the worst about her.

"Do you have anyone with a grudge against you?" Raleigh asked Yvette. "Someone who might want to try to kidnap the baby and hold her for ransom?"

Yvette was shaking her head before he even finished the question. "Of course not. My husband and I manage my late father's successful real estate company. We've never even had a serious complaint from a customer."

No, but that didn't mean someone hadn't kidnapped the baby for ransom. That's the reason Raleigh had told the woman to keep her phone close to her. Yvette had. In fact, she was doing everything a frantic mother would do to find her child. But something was missing here.

Or rather *someone.*

"Where's your husband?" Thea asked. "You called him right after we discovered the body, so shouldn't he have been here by now?"

Since Yvette was still looking a little defensive, Thea expected the woman to blast her for even hinting that Mr. O'Hara wasn't doing all he could to be there to comfort his wife or look for their child. But Yvette's reaction was a little surprising. She glanced away, dodging Thea's gaze.

Now, this was a red flag.

"Nick had some things to tie up at work," Yvette answered after several long moments.

Raleigh made one of those vague sounds of agreement. "Yeah, Sonya mentioned to me that your husband wasn't completely on board with having this baby."

Thea tried not to look too surprised, but she suspected that was a lie. She'd had a lot of conversations with Sonya, and never once had the surrogate brought up anything like that. If Sonya had, it would have been one of those red flags that Thea had been searching so hard to find.

What was equally surprising though was that Yvette didn't even deny it.

"Nick had a troubled childhood," Yvette said, still not looking at either Thea or Raleigh. She stared past them and into the yard. "He was hesitant about us having a baby because of all the money it would cost for a surrogate. And because of all the time I'd have to take off from the business to be a stay-at-home mom. But he finally agreed to it."

Maybe. And maybe Nick hadn't actually agreed the way that Yvette thought. It seemed extreme though to kill a surrogate so that he wouldn't have to be a father, especially since the baby had already been conceived. And born. Still, Thea would look into it, and she was certain Raleigh would, as well.

"Call your husband again," Raleigh told the woman. "I want him to come to the sheriff's office on Main Street in Durango Ridge in thirty minutes. I'll take Thea and you there now in the cruiser, and he can meet us."

Yvette started shaking her head again, and alarm went through her eyes. "He had nothing to do with this, and it'll only upset him if you start interrogating him the way you did me."

Thea had watched that so-called interrogation, and Raleigh had handled the woman with kid gloves. He'd treated her like a distraught mother whose child had been stolen. She doubted Raleigh would show that same consideration to Nick. Because Nick apparently had a motive for this nightmare that'd just happened.

Raleigh checked the time and motioned for Yvette to make the call. The woman hesitated, but she finally went to the other end of the porch to do that. Too bad Yvette didn't put it on speaker, because Thea would have loved to hear Nick's response to Raleigh's order.

While Yvette was still on the phone, Raleigh turned back to Thea. "I'll need you to give me a statement, of course." He hesitated, too. "And you should be in protective custody."

He was right, but it riled her a little that he thought she couldn't take care of herself. After all, she was a cop, and she could point out to him that the thug hadn't murdered her when he or she had the chance. Still, she needed to take some precautions.

Once Yvette had finished her call, Thea stood, ready to go to the cruiser, but she stopped when she heard the approaching vehicle. Raleigh and Dalton must have heard it, too, because they automatically stepped in front of her and Yvette. Thea slid her hand over the gun that she'd borrowed from Raleigh. But it wasn't the threat they were all obviously bracing themselves for.

It was Warren.

He pulled his familiar black truck to a stop behind the trio of cruisers and the other vehicles, and he got out and started for the house.

"What the hell is he doing here?" Raleigh asked, turning his glare back on Thea.

"I didn't call him," Thea said, but it would have been easy enough for Warren to hear about it. After all, most law enforcement agencies in the state had been alerted to the missing baby.

"Raleigh," Warren greeted. He obviously ignored the glare his son now had aimed at him, and he walked right past Raleigh to pull Thea into his arms.

It certainly wasn't the first time that Warren had hugged her. He'd always treated her like family and had practically raised her and her brother, Griff. But it felt awkward now in front of Raleigh—who hadn't gotten that same family treatment from the man.

"Are you okay?" Warren asked her when he pulled back from the hug.

His attention went to the stun gun marks on her neck, and it looked as if he had to bite back some profanity. When she'd been his deputy, he had always hated whenever she'd gotten hurt or been put in danger, and he still apparently felt that way. Thea appreciated the concern, especially since she'd never gotten any from her own parents, but it made the situation with Raleigh seem even more awkward.

"I'm fine," Thea assured him. She didn't

especially want to bring this up, but Warren would soon learn it anyway. "Whoever did this also took the newborn, and he left a message on the wall—"

"Two messages," Raleigh corrected. "There was a second in Sonya's bedroom. They were both written in red paint and used identical wording to what was left at Hannah's place. 'This is for Sheriff Warren McCall.'"

"This man is Sheriff McCall?" Yvette asked. Warren nodded, and she went to him, catching on to his arms. "Who did this? Why would someone take my baby because of you?"

Warren's face tightened. "I don't know."

"But you must have some—" Yvette started, but Raleigh moved her away when her grip tightened on Warren.

"This is the missing baby's mother," Raleigh explained. "Yvette O'Hara."

Warren tipped the brim of his Stetson as

a greeting. "I'm really sorry for what happened, but I honestly don't know who took your child." He turned to Raleigh. "Are you sure this is connected to Hannah, or is it a copycat?"

A muscle flickered in Raleigh's jaw. "Too early to tell. Do you have a reason for being here?" There definitely was nothing friendly about his tone.

Warren sighed. "Yes. I was worried about Thea and thought she might need a ride home because she's so shaken up."

"She will, but only after she's given her statement about the attack." Again, there was no friendliness from Raleigh. "I was about to take her to my office now. No reason that I know of for you to be there for that, but you can wait for her at the café across the street."

Warren would do that if he couldn't get Raleigh to relent and let him stay with her in the sheriff's office. And Raleigh wouldn't back down on this.

They started down the steps, and Thea didn't miss it when she saw Warren wince and slide his fingers over his chest. He quickly moved his hand away, but she knew he'd been touching the scar beneath his shirt. The scar he'd gotten from a gunshot wound six months ago.

The wound itself had healed, but the muscles there had been damaged enough that Warren would always have pain. Something he obviously didn't want to discuss because he shook his head when Thea opened her mouth to ask if he was okay. Maybe it was a guy thing not to want to admit that he was in pain, or maybe he just didn't want to talk about it in front of Raleigh.

"Ride in the cruiser with Raleigh," Warren whispered to her, and he made a lawman's glance around them. "There are a lot of places for a killer to lie in wait on the road that leads into Durango Ridge."

She nodded, but his reminder only gave her another jolt of adrenaline. So did the sound of her phone ringing. Not a reaction she wanted to have as a deputy. Nor was the reaction she had next.

Her stomach went to her knees when she looked at her phone screen.

"Unknown caller," she said.

That stopped Raleigh and Warren, and Yvette eventually stopped, too, when she realized they were no longer moving toward the cruiser.

It could be nothing, maybe even a telemarketer, but Raleigh must have realized it could be something important because he took out his own phone to record the call, and he motioned for her to answer it. She did, and unlike what Yvette had done earlier, Thea put it on speaker.

"I'm guessing you're looking for the kid," a man immediately said. Thea didn't recognize his voice, but it was possible that it was the same man who'd taken Sonya.

Yvette gasped, and Warren motioned for her to stay quiet. Good move because it wouldn't do any good to have Yvette start yelling at this thug.

"Where's the baby?" Thea demanded. Of course, she wanted to ask the snake why he'd murdered Sonya, but right now, the baby had to come first. It was too late to save Sonya, but maybe they could still help the child.

"I'll give her to you. All you have to do is come and get her."

Thea looked at Raleigh to get his take on this. Like her, he was clearly skeptical, but at the moment, this was all they had. Maybe it was a matter of paying a ransom. If so, she figured they could scrape together whatever amount they needed to get the child safely away from a killer.

The conversation must have alerted Dalton because he came down the steps and into the yard with them.

"Where's the baby?" Thea repeated to the man.

"I'll text you the time and the place where you can get her. Oh, and I'll text you the rules, too. Don't forget those or you won't get the kid." He sounded arrogant, and Thea wished she could reach through the phone and make him pay for what he'd done.

She tamped down the anger so she could speak. "How do I know you actually have her? This could be a trap."

"Sweetcakes, if I'd wanted you dead, you

already would be. You wouldn't have made it off that back porch of Sonya's house."

Since Thea had already realized that, she knew it was true. But there were plenty of other things that didn't make sense. "How do I know for certain that you have the newborn?" she pressed.

The man didn't answer. Not with words anyway. But Thea heard the sound in the background.

A baby crying.

Chapter Three

Raleigh cursed and snatched the phone from Thea. "Tell me the location of the baby now!" he demanded. But he was talking to the air, because the kidnapper had already ended the call.

"Oh, God." Yvette grabbed the phone, too, and she hit Redial.

No answer.

A hoarse sob tore from Yvette's mouth, and she would have likely fallen to the ground if Warren hadn't caught her. Raleigh didn't thank him for doing that because he didn't want the man anywhere around here. Raleigh had enough distractions with Thea and Yvette, and he didn't need to add his so-called father to the mix.

Raleigh turned to Dalton. "Take Yvette to the station. Call a doctor for her, too. She might need some meds to calm her down."

"The only thing I need is my baby!" Yvette shouted.

The woman tried Redial again, and she was gripping Thea's phone so hard that Raleigh thought she might break it. That wouldn't be good since it was obviously the way the kidnapper had chosen to communicate with them.

"She's a newborn," Yvette went on. "She has to be fed. Someone has to take care of her."

"And the men who have her will do that," Thea said. "They'll want to keep the baby safe and well. Remember, they took formula so she won't be hungry."

True, but that didn't mean a newborn was

going to get expert care from the thugs who'd snatched her. That's why they had to find her ASAP.

Dalton gently took Yvette by the arm. "Once we get to the station," he told the woman, "I'll examine the call. I might be able to get a match on his voice, because Raleigh will send me the recording of the conversation."

Raleigh would do that, but he wasn't holding out any hope for a match. Or that the call would be traced for that matter. The kidnapper had almost certainly used a burner cell, a disposable one that couldn't be traced. Still, they'd try.

"What can I do?" Warren asked him.

"You can go home to your wife and family in McCall Canyon until I've got time to interrogate you. After all, it was your name on that wall, and there had to be a reason for it."

That was a knee-jerk reaction. One that

Raleigh instantly regretted. Not because he hadn't meant it—he had. But it was the wrong time to vent.

Raleigh took a deep breath to steady himself. "My people have the scene secured," he added to Warren. There was much less emotion in his voice now, which was a good thing. "Give me a couple of hours so I can deal with this kidnapper, and then I can question you."

Warren didn't balk at any part of that, but judging from his tight expression, something was on his mind. "What about Thea?" Warren asked.

Of course. Thea. Warren was worried about the woman he'd practically raised.

"I'll take Thea to the station so we can wait on this thug to call us back," Raleigh answered.

Warren stood there, his hands on his hips while he volleyed glances between them as if he was trying to figure out if that was the wise thing to do. The man didn't budge until Thea nodded.

"I'll be okay," she assured Warren.

"Call me if you need anything," Warren finally said, and he hugged her again. After he pulled away from her, he looked at Raleigh, maybe trying to figure out what to say to him, but he settled for another tip of his hat. This one was a farewell, and he headed to his truck.

Raleigh and Thea were right behind him, and the moment Raleigh had her in the cruiser, he started toward town. It wouldn't be a long drive, only about twenty minutes, but he could use that time to get some things straight.

"The kidnapper said there'd be rules," he reminded her. "That probably means a ransom demand with instructions for the payout so we can get the baby. You won't be involved in that. If I haven't worked out a protective custody arrangement by then, you can wait in my office."

She shook her head. "The kidnapper said I was to come and get her."

"That won't be happening." At least he hoped not anyway. Raleigh didn't want to involve Thea in this any more than she already was.

But obviously Thea wasn't giving up. "I'm the person best suited to make an exchange like that. The kidnapper said if he wanted me dead, he would have killed me on the porch. And he could have done just that."

Raleigh wasn't giving up, either. "Maybe because the person standing next to you was holding a baby, and he didn't want to risk hurting her. That could have been the sole reason he didn't kill you."

She opened her mouth as if she might disagree with that, but she must have realized it could be the truth because Thea huffed and leaned back against the seat.

"I'll get Yvette's husband in for questioning," Raleigh added a moment later. "Right now, he's a person of interest. He could have orchestrated all of this because he doesn't want to be a father."

Though it did seem extreme—unless he hadn't intended for Sonya to die. Maybe the thugs hadn't had orders to kill Sonya or anyone else who showed up. That would explain why they'd had a stun gun with them. It would also explain why the one that Thea had seen was wearing a ski mask. He didn't want his identity known because he hadn't intended to kill any witnesses.

That was the best-case scenario though. It was still possible that the goons wanted Thea dead.

"Warren is a person of interest, too?" she asked.

"Of course." Raleigh would love nothing more than to charge the man with something. Anything.

"And what about your mother?" Thea pressed. "Will you also question her?"

Raleigh's gaze slashed to her, and he nearly had another of those knee-jerk reactions. But he forced himself to see this through her cop's perspective. His mother, Alma, no longer loved Warren. In fact, she might actually hate him.

"Alma thought Warren was going to leave his wife to be with her," Thea continued when he didn't say anything. "That didn't happen, and when he broke off things with her six months ago—"

"Don't finish that," Raleigh warned her. "I know how upset my mother was, and I don't have to hear a recap from you."

Hell, she was still upset. Alma had carried

on an affair with a married man, gotten pregnant and had basically lived her life waiting for the emotional scraps that Warren might toss her. Now that the secret was out, she was just seething in anger.

Raleigh hated to admit it, but he was seething, too. Because his mother had lied to him about his father. She'd lied all because she didn't want Warren's secret life exposed. Well, it was sure as hell exposed now.

"Did your mother know Sonya well?" Thea asked. It was a cop's kind of question, because Thea was again trying to link his mom to what was going on.

"Everyone in town knew Sonya," Raleigh snarled. But his mom had known Sonya better than most because Sonya had done some office work at his mother's ranch. "Don't worry. I'll question my mom," Raleigh added. "But there are plenty of other ways for her to get back at Warren. Ways that don't involve kidnapping a newborn baby and killing a surrogate."

It surprised him a little when Thea made a sound of agreement. After all, Warren's wife, Helen, had raised Thea, too, and that meant Thea and the McCalls likely thought of his mother as the villain in all of this.

"There doesn't seem to be a connection between Warren and Sonya," Thea added. "If your mother was going to try to get back at him in some way, she would go after him or someone he cared about."

True. But his mother would only do that if she'd finally gone off the deep end. There were times when Raleigh thought she might be headed there, and he was doing his damnedest to make sure that didn't happen.

"I also want to talk to the doctor who did the in vitro procedures for both Hannah and

Sonya," Raleigh continued, and he was about to ask Thea what she knew about the man, but her phone rang.

Unknown Caller.

Raleigh immediately pulled onto the shoulder of the road so he could again use his phone to record the conversation. Once he had it ready, Thea took the call. The first thing Raleigh heard was the baby crying again. It was like taking hard punches to the gut. It sickened him to think of these monsters having that little girl.

"All right, you ready to do this?" the kidnapper asked.

"We are," Raleigh answered, and he waited a moment to see if the guy would ask who he was. He didn't. Which meant the thug likely knew all the players in this. That wasn't much of a surprise since whoever was behind this had probably done their homework.

"Good. Because I'm gonna make this real easy. Transfer fifty thousand into the account number that I'm about to text to you."

In the grand scheme of things, fifty thousand wasn't much for a ransom demand, which made Raleigh instantly suspicious. Then again, maybe these guys just wanted some quick cash so they could make a getaway. After all, they were killers now, and if arrested, they'd be looking at the death penalty. Fifty would be more than enough to escape.

"If you do it right," the kidnapper went on, "it'll only take a couple of minutes at most for the money to show up. Then you can have the kid."

Raleigh huffed. "How do we know you even have the child? The crying we heard could be any baby. Or a recording. And if you do have her, what stops you from taking the money and running?"

"I figured you'd ask that. Well, I'm sending you a picture of the kid, and since Thea's using her cell for this call, I'll text it to your phone."

The guy didn't ask for Raleigh's number, and several moments later Raleigh's phone did indeed ding with a text message. Two of them, in fact. The first was the routing number for a bank account. Probably an offshore one that would be out of reach of law enforcement.

Raleigh went to the second text. A photo. It was indeed a baby wrapped in a blanket, and seeing her was like another punch. He reminded himself though that the picture could be fake. But this didn't feel like a ruse. Raleigh was certain these snakes had that little girl.

He showed the photo to Thea, and he saw the raw emotions go through her eyes. "Oh, God," she whispered, her voice mostly breath.

She obviously didn't think it was a ruse, either. And that led Raleigh back to his second issue with this ransom arrangement.

"I'll transfer twenty grand," Raleigh told the kidnapper. He could take that from his own personal checking account. "You'll get the rest when I actually see the baby. And Thea will have no part in the drop. It'll be between you and me."

Along with some backup deputies that Raleigh would have in place. The plan was to catch these idiots and make them pay for what they'd done. First though, he had to make sure the baby was safe.

The guy didn't say anything, and the silence went on for what seemed to be an eternity. "All right," the kidnapper finally answered.

"Get that money to me in the next five minutes, and then I'll give you the location of the kid."

Before Raleigh could ask for any more time, the kidnapper ended the call. Raleigh didn't bother to hit Redial because it would just eat up precious time.

He had a quick debate with himself as to how to handle this, and the one thing he knew was that he didn't want Thea anywhere near this. That meant getting her to the station.

"Call the emergency dispatcher," Raleigh said as he used his own phone to access his bank account. "Have him connect you to Dalton. Tell him to gather up as many deputies as he can because I might need them. I also need Dalton to get the remaining thirty grand of the ransom money." If nothing went wrong with the first part of this plan, Raleigh wanted to be ready.

"I could do backup," Thea insisted. "I still have your gun, and I'm not woozy anymore from the stun gun."

Raleigh dismissed that with a headshake and motioned for her to make the call. She did, and he continued with his own task.

It took several moments for him to get access to his account, several more for Raleigh to put in the number the kidnapper had given him. The transfer went through without any hitches.

He had more money in investment accounts, but he doubted those would be as easy to tap into. That's why he'd wanted Dalton to come up with the rest. That would involve getting some help from fellow law enforcement, maybe even the DA. Somehow though, they'd come up with that money.

"Dalton said to tell you that he'll get to work right away on all of that," Thea relayed to him the moment she finished her call. She also took his phone and had another look at the photo the kidnapper had sent. "I'm just trying to figure out if there's any resemblance between the baby and Yvette."

"And?" He started driving again so he could get Thea to the station. They were still ten minutes out, so Raleigh sped up. After everything that'd happened, he didn't want to be on this rural stretch of road any longer than necessary.

"I can't tell. You think we should send it to Yvette to see if she recognizes any features? The baby could resemble her husband since it was Yvette's and his fertilized embryo that was implanted in Sonya."

He had another short debate about that and dismissed it. The woman had been so frantic that this might push her over the edge. Raleigh wanted her to stay put with Dalton at least until he could get there.

"Egan would send backup if you need it," Thea reminded him.

She probably hadn't suggested that to rile him. After all, *Egan* was Sheriff Egan McCall of McCall Canyon. Along with being Thea's boss, he was Raleigh's half brother and Warren's son. Raleigh wasn't so stubborn that he would refuse help and therefore put the baby at even greater risk, but he didn't think he would have to rely on McCall help just yet.

Only a short distance ahead, Raleigh spotted a dark blue SUV. It wasn't on the road but had pulled off onto one of the ranch trails. A trail with a lot of trees and wild shrubs. Normally, seeing a vehicle parked there wouldn't have alarmed him. After all, there was pasture land out here for sale, and this could be a potential buyer. But this day was far from normal.

"You recognize the SUV?" Thea asked. She drew her gun, which meant this had put her on edge, too.

"No." And it was parked in such a way that he couldn't see the license plates.

Raleigh considered just speeding up, and once he passed the vehicle, he could get the plates and call them in. But he saw something else. Something on the ground next to the passenger's side door.

"Is that what I think it is?" Thea muttered. "It looks like a baby carrier."

It did. Raleigh had already had a bad feeling about this, and that feeling went up a significant notch when the SUV came flying off the trail and onto the road just ahead of Thea and him. The driver sped away, heading in the direction of town.

Raleigh hit his brakes and slowed so he could have a better look. At first, he thought the carrier was empty, that this was some kind of trick. But then he saw the baby's tiny hand moving away. He heard the cries, too.

His phone dinged with another text. Since Thea still had hold of it, she read it to him. "Change of plans. The kid is all yours. Thanks for the twenty grand."

Raleigh wanted to know what had happened to make them flee like that. He also wanted to go in pursuit, but that would mean leaving the baby out here.

"Call Dalton back," he told Thea. "Let him know what's happening. I want that SUV stopped."

While she did that, Raleigh drew his gun and got out. He fired glances all around them but didn't see anyone. However, the baby's cries seemed to be even more frantic now. She could be hungry or scared.

Still keeping watch, Raleigh went closer, and he prayed this wasn't some elaborate dummy. It wasn't. The baby was real. And there was what appeared to be a note on the blanket that was loosely draped over her.

Raleigh went to her, stooping down, and he touched her cheek, hoping to soothe her. It didn't work. She kept crying, and he was about to pick her up when he saw what was written on the note.

He read the note out loud, so Thea could hear. "'Warren's going to be so sad when he finds out she's dead.'"

Raleigh shook his head, not understanding what it meant. Who was the *she*? Certainly not the baby because she was very much alive. It hit him then. Another she, and this one was definitely connected to Warren. He whipped back around, his attention going to the cruiser.

What he saw caused his heart to go to his knees.

Because there was a guy wearing a ski mask, and he had a gun pointed right at Thea's head.

Chapter Four

Thea was certain that Raleigh was cursing her as he was diving for cover with the baby. She was cursing herself for letting this snake get the drop on her and knocking the gun from her hand. Yes, she was still wobbly from the other attack, but that was no excuse. She was a cop, and she shouldn't have let this happen.

Especially because it could end up getting Raleigh and the baby hurt.

Raleigh was obviously trying to prevent that from happening because he dropped down into the shallow ditch with the baby. It wouldn't be much protection if shots were fired, but it was better than being out in the open. And much better than having the baby in the hands of this thug.

She had no idea who was holding her at gunpoint, but one thing was for certain—if he'd wanted her dead, she already would be. Instead of grabbing her when she stepped from the truck, he could have just put a bullet in her head and then escaped. Raleigh would have had a hard time going after him with a baby in tow.

So, what did the thug want?

Thea prayed that whatever it was, the baby wouldn't be put in any more danger. The newborn had already been through enough.

"Why are you doing this?" Thea managed to ask.

It was hard for her to talk though because he had her in a choke hold, and the barrel of the gun was digging so hard against her skin that she'd probably have a fresh cut to go along with the one she'd gotten when she fell on Sonya's porch after being hit with the stun gun.

Was this the same attacker?

She didn't know, and even if she got a chance to see his face beneath that ski mask, she still probably wouldn't recognize him.

And that only left her with another question. Where was his partner? He had almost certainly been the one to drive away in the SUV—probably after this thug had gotten out and hidden in a ditch to wait for them. But the partner would come back. No doubt soon. That meant Raleigh and she didn't have much time.

"Let her go," Raleigh called out, though he certainly knew that wasn't going to stop this thug. However, he had positioned himself in front of the baby, and he had his gun ready.

Not that he had a shot.

The guy behind her was hunched down just enough that Raleigh wouldn't be able to shoot him. She certainly wouldn't be able to do that, either, not with the backup weapon that Raleigh had given her on the ground. She was only about five feet away from where it had fallen when the guy bashed his own weapon against her hand to send the gun flying. But despite it being that close, there wasn't much of a chance she could get to it without getting shot. Still, she would have to go for it if he tried to hurt the baby. First though, Thea wanted to know what the heck was going on.

"Did you bring the baby here?" she demanded, and she hoped she sounded a lot stronger than she actually felt. Thea was scared. Not for herself but for the baby.

"Nope. It wasn't me. But this is how this is going to work," the guy said in a voice plenty loud enough for Raleigh to hear. "First you're gonna use your phone to transfer the rest of the money. All thirty grand of it. Then, you're gonna bring the kid to me."

Raleigh cursed. "Why the hell would I do that?"

"Because if you don't, I'm gonna shoot this pretty lady here. Warren's going to be so sad if that happens."

It was similar wording to what had been in the note, but Thea didn't take either it or this snake's threat at face value. He could be lying so he could connect Warren to this. Of course, Thea didn't know why he would do that, but it was still a possibility. None of this had felt right from the beginning.

"Did Nick O'Hara hire you to do this?" she snapped. "Is that why you want the baby?"

The thug didn't answer, but she thought maybe he tensed more than he already was.

Hard to tell though because he was wired and practically fidgeting. Definitely not someone she wanted with his finger on the trigger.

"Transfer the money now!" he shouted to Raleigh.

Raleigh had his famous glare aimed at the thug, but she also saw him do something with his phone. Even though there hadn't been a lot of time to do it, maybe Raleigh's deputy had managed to get the money. If not, perhaps she could bargain with her captor to let her call Warren for the funds. That could also buy her some time so she could figure out what to do.

"Once you have me and the money," she said to the guy, "there's no reason for you to have the baby, too. She's a newborn, and she needs to be at the hospital."

"What the kid needs is for the sheriff to co-operate," he snarled. She felt him fumbling around and realized he was checking his phone. No doubt looking to see if the transfer had been made.

Raleigh lifted his head enough for Thea to make eye contact with him, and for a moment she thought he was going to say he hadn't been able to get the money. But the thug made a sound of approval.

"Good job," he told Raleigh. "I knew you'd come through for me."

Thea didn't breathe easier, because she figured what was coming next, and she didn't have to wait long for it.

"Now the kid," the guy said. "Me and Thea are going to walk closer to you to get her. That means you toss out your gun and keep your hands where I can see them."

"So you can kill me? I don't think so. Tell me, why didn't you just take the baby and run?"

"Oh, I will be doing that." He chuckled and

started walking with her. "First though, I had to fix a screwup."

Thea wasn't sure if he meant her or not. Maybe his partner and he thought she could ID them. She couldn't. But since a murder charge was on the table, they might not want to risk it. Or it could be something more than that. They could want to use her to get to Warren.

Or make it look as if they were using her for that.

She heard the sound of a car engine, and moments later the blue SUV came into view. It was creeping toward them, the driver probably looking to make sure his partner had what they'd come for—the baby and her. And in a few more seconds, that might happen if she didn't do something.

Raleigh still didn't have a shot, but since he still hadn't tossed out his gun, there was a chance that her captor would shift his position enough for Raleigh to take him out.

"Are you deaf?" the man shouted to Raleigh. "I told you to drop the gun."

There was no way Thea could let that happen, not with the SUV getting closer and closer. Right now the thug holding her was outnumbered, but that wouldn't be true once his partner arrived onto the scene.

She looked at Raleigh again, hoping that he was ready for what she was about to do. If not, it could get them both killed.

Thea dragged in a deep breath, and just as the thug pushed her forward another step, she rammed her elbow into his stomach. In the same motion, she dropped down her weight. She didn't get far though because he still had her in a choke hold.

But she did something about that, too.

Thea twisted her body, ramming him again

with her elbow until he loosened his grip enough for her to drop down low enough to give Raleigh a chance at a shot. She prayed it was one he would take.

And he did.

Raleigh already had his gun lifted, and the bullets blasted through the air. One shot, quickly followed by another.

Time seemed to stop. Thea thought maybe her heart had, as well. She could only wait to see what had happened, and several long moments later, the thug's grip on her melted away as he collapsed to the ground. She glanced back at him and saw the blood and his blank, already lifeless eyes. Raleigh's shot had killed him.

"Get down!" Raleigh shouted to her.

Thea scrambled away from the thug, snatching up the gun as she ran, and she dropped down into the ditch. It wasn't a second too soon. Because more shots came. Not from Raleigh this time but from the person who was in the SUV.

The bullets slammed into the surface of the road, just inches from where she was. That told her that she was the target since the shooter didn't try to take out Raleigh even though he also had a gun. But what she still didn't know was why this attack was even happening.

The gunman fired two more shots, both of them slamming into the dirt bank of the ditch just above her head. If he changed the angle just a little or got closer, he'd have a much easier time killing her. However, as bad of a thought as that was, at least this snake wasn't shooting in the direction of the baby.

Thea waited for a lull in the shooting, and she lifted her head enough to take aim at the shooter. He was wearing a ski mask and was leaning out of the driver's-side window. She fired right at him.

So did Raleigh.

She wasn't sure which of their bullets hit the windshield, but one slammed into the glass. It also sent the shooter ducking back into the SUV. Almost immediately, he threw the SUV into Reverse and hit the accelerator.

He was getting away.

Thea definitely didn't want that, because they needed him to get answers. She came out of the ditch, aiming at the tires, and she fired. The SUV was already moving too fast though, and before she could even take a second shot, it was already out of sight.

RALEIGH STOOD IN the doorway of the ER examination room while he waited for his deputy Dalton to come back on the line. If they got lucky, then maybe Dalton would tell him that the driver of that SUV had been caught and was ready for interrogation.

Because Raleigh very much wanted to question him.

Then he'd arrest him for not only murder and kidnapping, but also for the attempted murder of two law enforcement officers, as well.

Thea looked up at him, no doubt checking to see if he knew anything yet, but Raleigh just shook his head. He also kept watch in the hall and ER to make sure a gunman didn't come rushing in to try to finish what he'd started.

There was a lot to distract Raleigh though, and he knew he had to be mindful of that. Thea was holding the baby while Dr. Halvorson, the pediatrician, finished up his exam. An exam that Raleigh hoped would let them know that the baby was all right. It would be somewhat of a miracle if she was, considering the ordeal she'd been through. At least she was too young to know what was going on, but maybe she could still sense the stress.

And there was plenty of that.

Thea's face was etched with worry, and Raleigh was certain his was, too. Because as long as the shooter was at large, then they were probably still in danger. It was too much to hope that the shooter would have fled and had no plans to return.

The doctor pushed his rolling chair away from Thea and the baby, and he stood. Raleigh turned so he could see the doctor but also keep watch.

"She seems to be just fine," Dr. Halvorson said, causing Raleigh to release a breath of relief. "Of course, I'll still run tests to make sure nothing shows up."

The tests would include a blood sample that a nurse had taken from the heel of the baby's foot. The newborn had definitely made a fuss about that, and Raleigh didn't intend to admit that it'd put a knot in his stomach. But when Thea had given her the bottle that the hospital had provided, the little girl had drifted off to sleep.

Thea had had to collect the baby's clothes and diaper. Since the items could have fibers and such on them, they'd been sent to the crime lab, along with the infant carrier. Thankfully, the hospital had had newborn gowns, fresh diapers and a blanket.

"I'm guessing it'll be a problem if we admit her to the hospital?" the doctor asked.

Raleigh had to think about that for a second. "It would, but if she needs to be here, we'll make it work."

The doctor shook his head. "I don't see a reason to admit her other than for observation. She's a healthy weight—seven pounds, four ounces. No breathing issues or signs of injury."

That was somewhat of a miracle. Too bad Sonya hadn't gotten a miracle of her own.

"Are there any indications that the baby was born from a forced labor?" Raleigh asked the doctor. "Like maybe some kind of drug?"

"I doubt we'd be able to tell that from the newborn, but something like that might be in Sonya's body."

The doctor's voice cracked a little on the last word. That was because he knew Sonya. Most people in Durango Ridge did. And it was hard to lose one of their own. Especially to murder.

"Raleigh, you still there?" Dalton asked when he came back on.

"Yeah." And he stepped out into the hall. He didn't put the call on speaker, because he didn't want anyone who happened to walk by to hear any grisly details. That meant he'd have to fill Thea in on whatever he learned.

"The other deputies didn't catch the guy," Dalton said, sounding as frustrated as Raleigh felt. "The APB is out on the blue SUV, so someone might spot it and call it in."

That could happen, but it was beyond a long shot. There hadn't been any plates on the SUV, so they couldn't try to trace the vehicle. And by now, the driver could have either ditched it or else put on some plates so that it wouldn't draw any attention from law enforcement.

"What about Nick and Yvette O'Hara?" Raleigh asked. "Are they still at the station?"

"She is. I've got her in an interview room, and she's pitching a fit to leave to go to the hospital and see the baby. I told her she shouldn't be out and about, not with the killer at large, but she's insisting."

Raleigh couldn't blame her. All indications

were that this was Yvette's daughter, and she was acting the way a distraught mother would. Her husband though was a different story. "See if you can find someone to escort her here." The hospital was only a couple of minutes from the station, so maybe there wouldn't be enough time for a killer to take shots at her. "And get Nick in for questioning ASAP."

Though he figured Dalton already had a list of things that fell into that *as soon as possible* category.

"Will do. We ran the prints on the dead guy, and we got an ID," Dalton went on a moment later. "His name was Marco Slater. Ring any bells?"

Raleigh mentally repeated it a couple of times and came up blank. "No. Should it?"

"According to Slater's record, Warren McCall arrested him for an outstanding warrant on a parole violation. That happened shortly before Warren retired when Slater was driving through McCall Canyon. Warren apparently recognized him from his mug shots."

Now, that was luck. Well, unless Slater had been on parole because of a crime he'd committed in or around Warren's town. Either way, Slater could have a grudge against Warren, and that could be motive for what had gone on today.

"Text me a copy of Slater's record," he instructed Dalton. "Was there anything on the body to tell us why he went after Thea and the baby?"

"Nothing. The guy wasn't even carrying a wallet, and other than extra ammo and a burner cell, there wasn't anything in his pockets."

So he was probably a hired gun, but maybe the lab would be able to get something from the phone. "Anything new from the ME on Sonya?"

"Not yet, but he said he would call as soon as he had something."

Raleigh needed the info, especially if there was any fiber or trace evidence on the body that could lead them to the driver of that SUV. Or the person who'd put the dead guy up to kidnapping the baby and killing Sonya. The driver could be the boss or just another hired gun.

"How's the kid?" Dalton asked. "And where will you be taking her?"

"She's fine." But Raleigh didn't have an answer for the second question. Since she could still be a target, she would need to be in protective custody. Ditto for Thea and maybe even Yvette. "I'll get back to you on the details," Raleigh added before he ended the call.

He put his phone away and stepped back

into the doorway. Of course, Thea's attention went right to him. "The gunman got away."

"For now." He hoped like the devil that would change soon.

"I need to check on another patient," the doctor said. Maybe he sensed that Raleigh needed to talk business with Thea. "Let me know what your plans are for the baby."

He would—as soon as he figured it out.

"You look as if you've had a lot of experience with kids," Raleigh said to Thea while the doctor was clearing out.

"Several of my friends have babies." With the newborn cradled in her arms, she brushed a kiss on the baby's head but kept her attention on Raleigh. Since she was a cop, she obviously knew he'd been discussing the specifics of the case, and there were a couple of the specifics that he wanted to go over with her.

"Marco Slater is the dead guy who tried to kill us. You know him?" he asked.

Raleigh saw the instant recognition in her eyes. "Marco Slater," she repeated. "He had a run-in with Warren years ago. He was supposed to be serving a ten-year sentence."

Well, the guy had apparently gotten an early release. Raleigh would find out more about that when he had Marco's records. "Did Marco hate Warren enough to put together a scheme that involves murder?"

She shook her head. "I remember Marco resisting arrest, and he took a swing at Warren. That's why he ended up with some extra jail time. I don't remember Marco vowing to get revenge though."

Maybe the man hadn't said it, but that didn't mean he hadn't attempted it. It could tie everything up in a neat little package, and Raleigh might not have to investigate anyone else who could have a grudge against Warren.

Like Raleigh's mother.

"There's more," Raleigh went on. "The CSIs are going through Sonya's house, and they found a tape recorder. Apparently, she was recording her calls. Did she happen to mention anything about that?"

"No," Thea answered without hesitation. She paused though. "She did say she'd had a bad relationship a couple of years ago. Maybe the old boyfriend was harassing her or something."

Now it was Raleigh's turn to say, "No. She did have a relationship, and it didn't end especially well, but I know the guy, and he's moved on. He's married, and they've got a baby." Though it was an angle he would check just in case. "I've got one of my deputies skimming through the recording just to see if anything stands out. If not, then I'll go over them more closely tonight."

At least he would do that if he wasn't still dealing with the O'Haras and a kidnapper.

Thea looked up at him again. "I know you're anxious to put some distance between us," she said. "But I'd rather work on this investigation than be tucked away at a safe house, in protective custody."

Yes, he was ready for them not to be under the same roof, but Thea probably believed that was because of the bad blood between them. And there was indeed some of that. But the attraction was stirring again, and Raleigh definitely didn't have time to deal with it. However, he seriously doubted that this would be a situation of out of sight, out of mind. No, now that she'd come back into his life, it wouldn't be easy to forget what they'd once had together.

She kept staring at him, obviously waiting for him to agree or disagree about the safe house. But Raleigh didn't get a chance to say anything, because he heard hurried footsteps.

Someone was running toward them.

Raleigh automatically drew his gun, but the person rushing to the room wasn't armed. It was Yvette, and she was ahead of one of his deputies, Alice Rowe, who was trying to keep up with her. Alice had no doubt escorted the woman there.

"Where is she?" Yvette asked the moment she spotted Raleigh. "Is she all right? I need to see her."

"The baby's fine," Raleigh assured her, and he stepped back so that Yvette could come in.

Yvette didn't take him at his word. No good mother probably would have. She went straight to Thea. Thea glanced at Raleigh, probably to make sure it was okay for her to hand over the baby, and Raleigh nodded. He wouldn't allow Yvette to take the newborn from the room, but he could see no harm in Yvette holding her. Thea eased the baby into Yvette's waiting arms.

Much as Thea had done on the ride to the hospital, Yvette pulled open the blanket and checked the baby. The little girl opened her eyes and looked out for a moment before she went back to sleep.

"Oh, she's perfect," Yvette said, and tears filled her eyes. She ran her fingers over the baby's dark brown hair. "Please tell me those kidnappers didn't hurt her."

"They didn't," Raleigh assured her, and he was about to fill her in on what the doctor had said, but he heard Alice in the hall.

"Stop right there," Alice warned someone.

That sent Raleigh hurrying to see what had caused his deputy to say that, and he soon spotted the bulky, sandy-haired man trying to push his way past the deputy. "I'm Nick O'Hara," the man snarled. "I know my wife is here because I saw her come into the building. Where is she?"

"That's my husband," Yvette said on a rise of breath. She would have stepped out into the hall if Raleigh hadn't moved in front of her. "Stay put. One of the kidnappers is still at large, and he could come here."

That put a huge amount of concern in Yvette's eyes. She gave a shaky nod and stayed where she was. Raleigh stepped outside, his gaze connecting first with Nick and then with Alice. "Frisk him," he told Alice.

That earned him a glare from Nick, but Raleigh didn't care. Yvette had been checked for weapons when she'd been taken to the sheriff's office, and Raleigh wanted the same to happen to Nick.

"He's clean," Alice relayed when she'd finished patting him down, and she let go of the man so he could come into the room. Nick's glare was still razor-sharp when he looked at Raleigh and Thea. And the look continued when he turned to his wife.

"Nick," Yvette said, smiling. "It's our daughter. She's safe."

The man went closer, peering down at the baby's face, and he shook his head. "That's not our kid." He snapped back toward Raleigh. "I don't know what kind of game you're playing, but it won't work. You can't pass that kid off as mine."

Raleigh glanced at Yvette to see if she had a clue what her husband was talking about, but she seemed just as confused as Raleigh. Thea, too, because she huffed.

"What are you talking about?" Thea asked.

"This," Nick snarled, and he whipped his

phone from his pocket. He lifted it so they could see the picture of a baby on the screen. It was a blonde-haired newborn wrapped in a pink blanket.

Yvette shook her head. "Who is that? Why do you have that picture?"

"Because someone texted it to me about ten minutes ago. Probably the same person who called me from an unknown number a few seconds later and demanded a quarter-of-a-million-dollar ransom."

"A ransom?" Yvette repeated. "Why?"

Nick tipped his head to the baby in her arms. "Because that's not our kid." He took the little girl from his wife and handed her back to Thea. "The kidnappers still have our baby, and we need to find her now."

Chapter Five

Thea had been so sure that Raleigh and she would have answers by the time they left the hospital, but that hadn't happened. And to make matters worse, they had to deal with the possibility that the O'Hara newborn was still out there.

In the hands of kidnappers.

But if that was true, then whose baby was in Thea's arms?

Thea was hoping they'd learn that now that they were at the sheriff's office. Yvette clearly wanted to know the same thing, and for the past hour since they'd left the hospital, she'd kept eyeing the child as if she might snatch her back from Thea. Since Yvette had been giving her that same look from the moment her husband had delivered that bombshell, Thea doubted the woman would try to take the baby and run. Still, she was keeping watch just in case. Yvette definitely looked ready to come unglued.

Thankfully, the baby was staying calm. Now that she'd been fed and changed anyway. Thea had done that as well, figuring that she was perhaps the only person in the building who'd actually had any experience doing it. Plus, she wanted to do it. It felt safer having the baby next to her.

"If the kidnappers really had our daughter, they would have called back by now," Yvette muttered.

That wasn't the first time she'd said something similar, and like the other times, her husband ignored her. Instead, Nick kept his attention on Dalton, who was setting up a recording device in the squad room. A recorder that would be used when and if the kidnappers called back. Before that, Nick had been on the phone, working out arrangements for a loan from Yvette's grandfather. The grandfather had agreed, though the man was apparently too frail to come to Durango Ridge to give his granddaughter some emotional support.

Something that Yvette seemed to definitely need.

Thea knew how she felt. She was still on edge from the attack and Sonya's murder, but she had to tamp down her nerves and focus on the investigation. Just as Raleigh was doing. He had his phone sandwiched between his shoulder and ear as he spoke to someone at the lab. While he was doing that, he was also checking something on his computer.

Thea wanted to help, but Raleigh had already made it crystal clear that she was not to let the baby out of her sight, or arms. He'd been insistent, too, that she stay away from the windows in case their attacker returned. Thea had had no problem with that, but it was the reason that she—and therefore Yvette and Nick—had ended up in Raleigh's office.

Soon though—very soon—they'd need to figure out if this second ransom demand was some kind of hoax. The baby in the photo Nick had shown them could be anyone's child, and this could be an attempt to milk the O'Hara's out of all that money. If so, it might work, too, since it was obvious that Nick and Yvette were planning on paying the demand.

When Raleigh finished his latest call, he brought his laptop to where Thea was seated, and he sank down in the chair next to her. "I had to have Alice call social services to tell them about the baby," he said, looking down at the newborn. "They're on the way here to take her."

That hit her a lot harder than Thea had expected, though Raleigh was right. There had been no choice about contacting them.

"What?" Yvette questioned. "You can't let them take her. Not until we're sure she's not ours."

"It's the law," Raleigh explained, "now that the baby's identity is in question."

Yvette shook her head and moved as if to take the baby, but her husband stepped in front of her. "This child has parents out there," he said. "Parents who are probably looking for her."

That was true, but there were no other missing baby reports. As a cop, that made Thea think the worst because if there was indeed a second baby, then the kidnappers could have murdered the parents when they took the child.

"But she could stay here with us until we sort it all out," Yvette argued. "And what about her safety? Can they protect her?"

"They know there's potential danger and will bring in the marshals." Raleigh paused, groaned softly. "It's out of my hands."

Apparently, it had hit Raleigh hard, too. But a police station was no place for a newborn. Especially when they had no idea if she was even a target.

More tears sprang into Yvette's eyes. Obviously, she didn't want this baby out of her sight, but she quit arguing and sank back down into the chair.

"The courier arrived at the lab with the DNA swabs," Raleigh added a moment later. "It'll be a day or two though before we have the DNA results on the baby."

That wasn't a surprise, though Thea wished they could have them sooner. Yvette probably felt the same way. Maybe even Nick, too, since he hadn't protested about giving a sample of his DNA, even though he seemed pretty certain that this little girl wasn't his child.

Once Yvette had her attention back on her husband, Raleigh shifted the laptop so Thea could see the screen, and she immediately saw Marco's records. "He did get an early release," Raleigh pointed out. "He's been out nearly a month now."

Plenty of time to plan the attacks, the kidnapping and even Sonya's murder. But had he done that? Marco certainly had a criminal history. Four arrests for breaking and entering, robbery and even assault. Those were serious enough charges, considering they showed a pattern of illegal behavior, but nothing on the rap sheet jumped out that this man could be a killer.

Of course, maybe Sonya's murder hadn't been planned. Heck, maybe Marco hadn't even had a part in that if it had been premeditated. Everything was in question now because of the second ransom demand.

"Did Marco have the funds to put together something like this?" she asked.

Raleigh lifted his shoulder and set his laptop aside. "If he did, he had it stashed away somewhere, maybe even under an alias. But it wouldn't have taken that much cash—not really. The SUV could have been a rental—Alice is checking on that now. And the driver could have been one of Marco's cronies who was working for a share of the first ransom."

A ransom that he didn't get because the FBI had managed to freeze the account where Raleigh had transferred the money. That was good that he wouldn't be out any cash.

"Dr. Bryce Sheridan is coming in first thing tomorrow morning," Raleigh went on. "I spoke to him briefly, and he claims he only did Sonya and Hannah's in vitro procedures, that he had no contact with either of the women once they were pregnant."

Thea thought about that a moment. "But you're bringing him in anyway?"

"This is a murder investigation. We're in *leave no stone unturned* territory." He paused. "That's why my mother is coming in tomorrow, as well. Sonya worked for her for a while. You didn't know?" he asked, no doubt when he saw the surprise in her eyes.

Thea shook her head. "Sonya didn't mention it."

"It was a few years ago. I'm not sure exactly

why Sonya quit or even if she was fired, but those are questions I need to ask my mother."

Apparently, he didn't want to do that unofficially, either, because it could make it seem as if he was giving her preferential treatment.

Nick's phone rang, the sound immediately getting everyone's attention. Raleigh and Yvette stood, and Dalton put his finger on the record button. But Nick shook his head when he glanced at the screen.

"Sorry, it's a business associate," Nick grumbled, and he let the call go to voice mail as he turned toward Raleigh. "Is this normal for the kidnappers to wait so long before calling back?"

Raleigh shrugged. "They could be doing this to put you even more on edge. Their logic could be the more frantic and desperate you are, the more you'll cooperate."

Thea hoped that was what was going on,

but this didn't feel right. The O'Haras could pay the ransom only to discover the newborn with them was their child after all.

There were sounds of voices in the squad room, and Raleigh stepped in front of Thea and the baby. Protecting them again. But Thea realized this wasn't a threat when she recognized one of the voices. Her brother, Texas Ranger Griff Morris.

Thea got up and went to the door to look out, and she immediately spotted not only Griff but another familiar face. Rachel McCall Morris. Rachel wasn't only Griff's wife though.

She was also Warren's daughter and Raleigh's half sister.

There was a marshal standing behind her, and Thea made the connection then. Rachel was a social worker, and she'd come here to take the baby.

"Raleigh," Griff greeted.

They'd met when Thea and Raleigh were dating, but Thea wasn't sure if Raleigh knew Rachel or not. Apparently, he did because he pulled back his shoulders and looked past Griff to stare at her.

The family resemblance was definitely there between the two, and Thea figured if there was anyone in the McCall family who could start mending the rift, it was Rachel. She looked like his kid sister. Plus, she was four months pregnant.

"I volunteered to do this," Rachel said, walking closer. She kept her eyes locked with Raleigh, too.

Even though Rachel and she were close friends, Thea could only guess what was going on in Rachel's mind. Part of her probably resented Raleigh because he was proof of Warren's affair, but then Rachel wasn't exactly on friendly terms with her father after news of that affair had ripped their family apart.

Rachel went to her, tearing her gaze from Raleigh so she could look at the baby. "Are you okay?" Rachel whispered to Thea, and she gave her a gentle hug.

"I've had better days," Thea whispered back.

Griff came to the doorway of the crowded office, and he took in everything with a sweeping glance before his attention settled on her. He didn't hug her, but Thea could see the concern in his eyes. Followed by the relief that she was okay.

"Anything from the kidnappers yet?" Griff asked.

She shook her head and gently transferred the baby to Rachel's arms. Yvette was right there, watching their every move. And still crying.

"Can't you just wait with her here?" Yvette asked. "We might know something soon."

Soon was being optimistic. Rachel and the rest of them knew that. "We'll take good care of her, I promise. She'll be under guard from Marshal McKinney and a Texas Ranger."

Yvette wiped some tears from her cheek. "Where will you take her?"

Rachel looked at Griff to answer that. "To a safe house. And no, I won't be able to tell you the location," he added before Yvette could ask. "We'll keep Sheriff Lawton informed though, and if anything develops, I'm sure he'll pass it on to you."

It wasn't much of a surprise that Yvette didn't seem pleased about that, either, and Raleigh must have decided it was best not to have the woman around when Rachel and the others actually left with the baby.

"Go ahead and take the O'Haras and the

recorder to the break room," Raleigh instructed Dalton. "Have the diner bring them over something to eat, too."

Of course, Yvette protested that, saying she didn't want to leave and that she wasn't hungry, but her husband put his arm around her waist to get her moving. Yvette kissed the little girl, but her husband barely spared the baby a glance before Dalton led them away.

"I'm guessing Nick O'Hara thinks there's no chance that this baby is the one their surrogate delivered?" Griff asked Raleigh.

"It appears that way." Raleigh kept his hard stare on Nick until he was out of sight. "Either that or he's a jerk. I'm not sure which yet. Yvette admitted that he was having second thoughts about fatherhood."

That caused Griff to mumble some profanity.

Rachel adjusted the baby's blanket while she

stepped closer to her brother. She opened her mouth and then closed it as if she'd changed her mind about what to say. "I'm glad Thea and you weren't hurt," Rachel finally said.

Raleigh nodded. Stared at her. Then he huffed. "Thanks for coming."

Even though the conversation was only a handful of words, it seemed to have set some kind of truce in motion. One that Thea was thankful for. It was a start, but she wasn't under any illusions that this would repair what she'd once had with Raleigh. No. Rachel hadn't known about her father's affair until it had come to light after his shooting. But Thea had known. And she'd kept it a secret. That was something Raleigh might never be able to get past.

When Rachel moved to the side, Griff came closer to Thea, giving her a once-over. The kind of look that only a big brother could manage. He respected her wishes to be a cop, but that didn't mean he didn't worry about her.

"You'll make sure she's okay?" Griff said to Raleigh.

Thea huffed and tapped her badge.

Griff huffed and motioned toward the stun gun marks on her neck.

She wanted to remind him that there were times when he'd been hurt, too, in the line of duty, but she didn't want to get into an argument with her hardheaded brother. Instead, she hugged him and gave the baby a goodbye kiss on the cheek.

Rachel turned to go but then stopped and looked at Raleigh again. "Maybe when this is over, we can meet for lunch or something. And yes, I know you don't like or trust us," she added before Raleigh could speak. "But I'm just as upset about what our father did as you are."

"Does that mean we're on the same side?" Raleigh asked, and it had some sarcasm in it. Some of the old wounds, too.

"Yes," Rachel said without hesitation. "And even if we weren't, we're still kin." She smiled and followed Griff out of the room.

"I don't need a family. Or siblings," Raleigh grumbled.

He didn't, but he had them whether he wanted them or not. Besides, one of those siblings might be able to help them with this investigation.

"Egan has the old case files on Hannah's murder," Thea reminded Raleigh. "If Sonya's murder is connected to hers, then it might not hurt to go through everything again." She paused, waiting for him to answer, but when he didn't say anything, she added, "I can ask Egan to send a copy here."

"No." That time Raleigh didn't hesitate. "I'll

ask him myself. But you've read everything in Hannah's file. Other than using the same doctor, do they have anything concrete in common?"

Obviously, he was putting aside the nearly identical threats left at Sonya's and Hannah's crime scenes. The threat that mentioned Warren. Thea wanted to put it aside, too, for now anyway, since the latest one could be a ploy to throw them off track.

"No," she answered. "But maybe Dr. Bryce Sheridan is behind this. Maybe there was something illegal going on at the fertility clinic, and he wanted to cover it up?"

Raleigh made a sound of agreement so quickly that he'd obviously already considered that. "But the murders happened a year apart. That's a long time for Dr. Sheridan to wait to cover up something. Unless, of course, he's committed several different crimes." He tipped his head toward the break room. "Right now though, Nick's high up on my list of persons of interest."

She agreed. The man certainly seemed to be anxious to hear from the kidnappers, but it also felt like there was an emotional disconnect. He could be that way though because his marriage was falling apart over his wife's insistence on having a child.

Raleigh dragged in a long breath. "I need to get back to Marco's rap sheet, and then I can make arrangements for a place for you to stay. Unless you want me to take you to the McCall Ranch."

"No." She didn't have to even think about that. "If the gunman that was in the SUV comes after me again, I don't want him to follow me to the ranch. Warren's still recovering from his injuries, and he could get killed trying to protect me."

She wanted to kick herself for putting it that way. It had to be a reminder that Warren had never done anything for Raleigh other than keeping the secret that he was his father. Raleigh had learned the truth about that only after Warren's affair with Raleigh's mother had been exposed.

"You have several people willing to protect you," Raleigh said.

She looked up at him just as he looked down at her. "Yes. But don't listen to what Griff told you. There's no need for you to make sure I'm okay." She added that just in case Raleigh considered himself one of those *several people.*

He continued to stare at her, and that's when Thea realized she was probably standing too close to him. She went to step back, but he took hold of her arm, keeping her in place.

"I think your brother was smart to tell me what he did," Raleigh said. "I believe you're in danger. I believe the driver of that SUV will come after you again. Why, I don't know, but Marco made it pretty clear that you were the target. And even if you're the target only to make us believe it's connected to Warren, that won't stop you from being gunned down."

She knew that, of course, but it sent a chill through her to hear it spelled out like that. Thea hadn't meant for her mouth to tremble and definitely hadn't wanted Raleigh to see it.

"Just because you're a cop, it doesn't mean you shouldn't be scared," he went on. "You should be. And while I understand you not wanting to go to the McCall Ranch so you can keep Warren safe, you'll need to be someplace where you have backup."

Thea clamped her teeth over her bottom lip for just a moment until she could regain her bearing. "I could go back to my office." Egan would make sure she had someone to help protect her, and he would do that even if it stretched his manpower thin. "Then I could come back in the morning when you question your mother and the doctor."

"You'll need a protection detail for the drive back and forth, too."

More manpower. But Raleigh's tone seemed to suggest something else. "You don't want me here for the interviews?"

"No. I do. You know more about Hannah's case than I do, and you know Warren. You might hear something that helps us figure this out." He paused, groaned softly. "If and when we eventually make it out of here tonight, you could stay at my place. It's not far."

"With you?" she blurted out.

The corner of his mouth lifted, but the slight smile didn't last long. "We're former lovers. I can't change that. But I don't want it to get in the way of us doing what needs to be done."

Neither did she, but Thea had to give this

some more thought. She'd been to Raleigh's horse ranch and knew his mom wouldn't be there. Alma had her own home and ranch just up the road from his. But still, she'd be under the same roof, and the attraction between them was still there. It was for her anyway.

Thea was so caught up in her own thoughts that the sound of the knock behind her nearly caused her to gasp. She whirled around, but it wasn't the threat that her body had believed it might be. It was Raleigh's deputy Alice, and even though the deputy didn't pose any danger, Thea could tell from her expression that something was wrong.

"Raleigh, you need to hear this." Alice was carrying a laptop that she sat on Raleigh's desk. "I had all of Sonya's recordings of her phone conversations transferred to an audio file that I could share with the lab, and I found something."

That definitely got Thea's and Raleigh's attention.

"It's the last one Sonya recorded," Alice continued. "Unfortunately, they're not date stamped, and she doesn't mention a date or time, so I don't know when the call came in."

Thea and Raleigh both moved closer to the laptop when Alice pressed the play button. It didn't take long for Thea to hear Sonya's voice.

"I swear I didn't know," Sonya said, her voice trembling. "I went in for the in vitro, and I thought that's what I got."

The sense of dread washed over Thea. Because obviously something had gone wrong at the clinic. Or at least Sonya thought something had.

"I'm not sure I can go through with this," Sonya went on. "Now that I know the baby is actually mine, how could I give her up?"

Oh, mercy. Yes, something had indeed gone wrong, and Raleigh was clearly just as stunned as she was.

"Who is she talking to?" Raleigh asked Alice.

But it wasn't necessary for the deputy to answer because the person spoke.

"We had an agreement," the other woman snapped. Thea easily recognized her voice, too.

It was Yvette.

"You're not backing out of our deal," Yvette insisted. "I've paid you plenty of money, thousands, and I'm not going to be punished because the clinic messed up." Unlike Sonya's voice, Yvette's wasn't shaking, but the anger came through loud and clear. "One way or another, Sonya, you will give me that child."

Chapter Six

At least Raleigh didn't have far to go to confront Yvette with what he'd just heard. And he would confront her and demand to know what the heck was going on.

With Thea and Alice right behind him, he went to the break room, where he immediately spotted Dalton and Nick seated at the table. Yvette was pacing, and her gaze zoomed to them when Raleigh stepped into the room.

"Did the kidnapper call you?" she blurted out. She continued to study his expression. "Oh, God. Did something happen to the baby?"

"The baby's fine," Raleigh assured her, "but I'm thinking you might want to have your lawyer come out here."

Yvette pulled back her shoulders. "What are you talking about?"

"This," he said. Raleigh had the laptop in his hands, and he rewound the recording to the last part of the conversation.

One way or another, Sonya, you will give me that child.

Yvette gasped and stormed toward him as if she were about to take the laptop, but Raleigh handed it to Thea in case he had to restrain Yvette.

"Where did you get that?" Yvette demanded. It was the same angry voice she'd used to threaten Sonya.

Before Raleigh asked her anything, he read Yvette her rights. Obviously, that didn't go over well, and her husband went to her side.

"What's this all about?" Nick asked as he volleyed glances between Yvette and Raleigh.

Raleigh just waited for Yvette to answer.

"Oh, God." Yvette pressed her fingers to her mouth a moment. And she started crying again.

But those tears didn't have the same heart-tugging effect they'd had on him earlier. Judging from Thea's huff, she felt the same way.

"Sonya recorded your whole conversation," Raleigh told the crying woman.

That wasn't exactly the truth. It was only a partial recording. Since Yvette didn't know that though, he was hoping she'd fill in the blanks. Maybe along with confessing that she was the one who'd set up this deadly chain of events.

"What's going on," Nick growled, and this time the demand was aimed at his wife. "What did you do?"

Yvette snapped toward him, her eyes suddenly wide. She started shaking her head. "I didn't kill Sonya if that's what you're suggesting."

"Then what the hell did you do?" Nick asked, taking the question right out of Raleigh's mouth.

Even with all of them staring at her and waiting, Yvette didn't answer right away. Still shaking her head, still crying, she sank down into the chair. "Sonya called me this morning and told me she'd found out something."

She looked up at Raleigh as if pleading with him not to make her explain this, but he motioned for her to keep talking. But Yvette had already given him something critical. The timing of the call. It meant the call could have been the trigger for Yvette to send in kidnappers to get the baby.

Yvette swallowed hard before she continued.

"Sonya said she got an anonymous tip that there'd been a serious mix-up when she had the in vitro procedure. The person claimed that my stored eggs were lost prior to fertilization, so the clinic decided to do an artificial insemination on Sonya instead."

Raleigh watched Nick as he processed that. It took him several long moments. "Are you saying the baby is Sonya's?"

Yvette nodded. "And yours. The baby is yours," she quickly repeated. She got to her feet and took hold of his arms when he cursed and tried to move away. "It doesn't matter to me that she's not my biological child. I'll still love her. We can still have the child we've always wanted."

Nick cursed some more and threw off her grip with more force than necessary. "A child *you've* always wanted," he corrected in a snarl.

He groaned, squeezed his eyes shut and put his hands on the sides of his head.

The man was clearly shaken by this and was probably seeing the irony. He hadn't especially wanted a child but had apparently fathered one. And Yvette wasn't the biological mother.

It took several more moments for the shock to wear off enough for Nick to whirl back around and face his wife. "What did you do? Did you hire those kidnappers?"

"No!" Yvette certainly didn't hesitate, and she repeated the denial to Thea and Raleigh. "I was upset when I said that to Sonya, but I would have never done anything to hurt the baby or her."

Maybe. But Raleigh still wasn't convinced. "Are there two babies?"

"I don't know. I swear, I don't."

Raleigh had to add another unspoken *maybe*

to that. "Who told Sonya about what had gone on at the clinic?"

"I told you already that it was an anonymous tip. Whoever it was sent her results of an amniocentesis to prove it. That's a test of the amniotic fluid around the baby. It can tell if there's something wrong." Yvette swallowed hard again. "And it can also tell the baby's DNA."

Interesting. Raleigh looked at Thea to get her take on this, and she was staring at Yvette. "Why was a test like that done? Was Sonya having medical problems?"

"She'd got an infection early on in the pregnancy, and the fertility clinic had her do the test just to make sure. We never heard back from them, so we assumed all was well."

That didn't mesh with what Dr. Sheridan had told them, that he hadn't had any involvement with Hannah or Sonya after the in vitro procedures. That was almost certainly a lie, one that Raleigh would definitely question him about. But it was possible that someone else in the clinic was responsible for the test and the botched procedure.

"I can't believe you didn't tell me this," Nick said, the anger etched all over his face. "And now Sonya's dead, and we don't know where the hell her baby is. *My baby*," he emphasized.

Yeah, and they didn't know if Yvette was responsible. It was time to move this past the chatting stage and make it a full-fledged interview. Before Raleigh did that though, he wanted to talk to Dr. Sheridan, and as late as it already was, that wasn't going to happen until morning.

"We're holding you for questioning," Raleigh told Yvette. "You aren't leaving the sheriff's office until I have some answers."

"Uh, you want me to put her in a holding cell?" Dalton asked.

If Nick was the least bit concerned about that happening, he didn't show it. In fact, he was looking at his wife with disgust. However, Yvette was definitely concerned.

"But I didn't do anything wrong," she practically shouted.

"You obstructed justice by not telling me the truth in a murder investigation," Raleigh explained. "The murder of a woman you hired as a surrogate. And now I have a recording of you arguing with that very woman just hours before she was killed."

"I didn't kill her." Now it was a shout, and she repeated it to her husband.

Nick huffed again. "You lied to me, too," he said after getting his teeth unclenched. "Hell, you even gave the cops a DNA sample to compare to the baby they found. You did that even though you knew you weren't going to be a match."

She tried to take hold of him again, but he pushed her away. "I thought once you learned the child was yours, that you'd love her. And that we would still be able to raise her. It doesn't matter that she's not a child of my own blood. She would have been *our* child. She still can be."

The anger tightened Nick's face so much that it was obvious he was having trouble reining in his temper. He cursed, groaned and went to stand in the doorway. "I don't even know if there's another baby. Or any real kidnappers." He kept going despite Yvette's continued denials. "Is there somewhere else I can wait for a kidnapper's call? Someplace where my *wife* won't be?"

Well, at least the man was willing to hang around in case there truly was a kidnapper.

At this point, Raleigh had no idea if there was one, or if this was part of Yvette's scheme to cover up her crime.

But that didn't make sense.

If Yvette had hired thugs to murder Sonya, then why would there be a second baby? Maybe the thugs had gone rogue and were now trying to milk as much money out of this situation as possible.

"Do you and your wife have joint bank accounts?" Raleigh asked Nick.

Nick nodded. For a moment it seemed as if he was going to ask why, but then his mouth tightened. "You want to examine them to see if she withdrew funds for this nightmare that's going on. Well, you're welcome to do that. I'll get you the account numbers and the passwords. In the morning, I'll call the bank and tell them you can have access to our safe-deposit box. There should be some family jewelry and cash in there."

He figured it was Nick's anger at his wife that was making him so cooperative, but Raleigh was thankful for it. This would save him from getting a court order and a search warrant.

"Take Mr. O'Hara to an interview room," Raleigh instructed Dalton. "Set up the recorder in there in case a kidnapper does call. The night deputies will be in soon so you can turn things over to them."

Dalton nodded, immediately picked up his equipment and started leading Nick out of the break room. Yvette didn't follow, but she did start sobbing again.

"Keep her here and instruct the night deputies to lock her up if she tries to leave," Raleigh added to Alice, and then he turned to

Yvette. "Remember that part about you having a right to an attorney. You might need it."

Since that only caused Yvette's sobbing to get worse, Raleigh led Thea back to his office. "You really believe she had Sonya killed?" Thea asked.

"Maybe. And maybe not intentionally." He glanced at Alice's laptop. "I want to go through all the recordings Sonya left. I need to know who gave her that anonymous tip. I'd also like to see if there's something to prove why she started the recordings in the first place."

While he was at it, Raleigh was also hoping he could find a connection between Yvette and Marco. The bank records could possibly help with that. If not, at least he would know if there'd been any recent cash withdrawals that Nick couldn't account for. If there was something like that, then it would be another circumstantial piece of evidence against Yvette.

"How much did Sonya know about Hannah's murder?" Raleigh asked Thea. "Did she know about the message that'd been left at the crime scene?"

There was no need for him to clarify which message because it was no doubt etched in their memories. *This is for Sheriff Warren McCall.*

Thea's forehead bunched up a moment while she gave that some thought. "Probably. When I told Sonya about Hannah and her using the same doctor, Sonya did an internet check to see if there were any other similarities between them."

Then yes, Sonya would have known about the message and could have mentioned it to Yvette. Yvette, in turn, could have had her hired henchmen write that on Sonya's wall to throw suspicion off herself. But there was plenty of suspicion on the woman right now.

Thea tipped her head to the laptop. "If you get me a copy of Sonya's audio recordings, I can go through them, too. I might hear something that I can connect to a conversation I had with her."

Good idea. They could work on that until they found out if Yvette's lawyer was going to show tonight. If he did, then he could start the interview. He still had the kidnapper-ransom issue to deal with, too, if the guy ever called back.

"I'll get you a laptop and the recordings," Raleigh said, heading out of his office.

With a deputy still at Sonya's house and with Dalton and Alice tied up, that only left him with two deputies in the squad room, Miguel Sanchez and Zeb Hooper. Miguel had his phone in his hand, and he was already making his way to Raleigh.

"Sheriff Egan McCall just found an abandoned vehicle on the outskirts of McCall Canyon," Miguel said. "It's a blue SUV matching the description of the one used in your attack."

Good. Because now they could process it for any evidence. Though he doubted it was a coincidence that the vehicle had been found in Warren's town. No. This could be another attempt to connect the murders to him.

Or maybe there really was a connection.

If so, Raleigh needed to find it before Thea and he landed again in the path of a would-be killer.

"There's more," Miguel added a moment later. "There was a dead body in the SUV, and according to his ID, it's someone you know."

Miguel handed him a note with the name, and the moment Raleigh saw it, he cursed.

Hell.

THEA WISHED SHE could turn her mind off for just a couple of seconds. She was exhausted from the spent adrenaline, the late hour and the events of the day, but she couldn't stop the thoughts from coming.

Another body.

And this time, it was Dr. Bryce Sheridan. He'd died from a single gunshot wound to the head that appeared to be self-inflicted.

Appeared.

Egan wasn't convinced it was a suicide though, and therefore neither was Thea. Egan was a good cop, and he had probably seen something with the positioning of the body or the gun that had made him believe this could be a setup.

Until Egan had found the body in the SUV, the doctor had been a person of interest in Sonya's murder. He was also someone that Raleigh and she had counted on to give them answers about Sonya's botched in vitro. But now that he was dead, they would have to wait until morning to get into the fertility clinic so they could access anything they could find.

Maybe before then, Raleigh and she could even manage to get some sleep. But Thea immediately dismissed that notion when she stepped into Raleigh's house. A different set of thoughts hit her then.

Scalding-hot memories of the nights she'd spent here with Raleigh.

Great. Just what she didn't need when she already felt so beaten down from the fatigue. So she had no choice but to stand there and let the memories run their course. Even when the most vivid images and sensations faded though, the thoughts still lingered.

Raleigh had kissed her right in the foyer. That'd been the start of some frantic foreplay that had led them straight to his bed. In those days, their whole relationship had seemed frantic. As if they were starved for each other and couldn't get enough. But that had all come crashing down when Raleigh had found out she'd kept Warren's secret about the affair.

And the secret that he was Warren's son.

When Thea's hand started to hurt, she glanced down and realized she had a too-tight grip on the overnight bag that Griff had packed for her and then sent to Raleigh's office. A bag that hopefully contained the things on the list she'd given him since she'd need a change of clothes and toiletries.

Too bad the bag wouldn't contain something to make her immune to Raleigh.

And speaking of Raleigh, he came in behind her, closing the door and setting the security system. He looked at her, and maybe because he saw something in her eyes, there was suddenly some alarm in his expression. Then he got it.

"Oh," he grumbled. "Yeah."

Thea could practically see the wall he'd just put up between them. A wall that hadn't been there as they'd worked together on the recordings and while waiting for the kidnapper to call back.

A call that hadn't come.

But now that they were back here, at the scene of their affair, then he probably knew it wasn't a good idea for them to be so chummy. With the attraction still simmering between them, even chumminess could lead to sex. Heck, maybe breathing could.

Another couple that definitely wouldn't be getting chummy tonight was Nick and Yvette.

Nick had refused to leave the sheriff's office because he wanted to be there in case the kidnapper did call. Since her lawyer wasn't arriving until morning, Yvette was still in the break room, where she'd stay until Raleigh either released her or charged her with obstruction of justice. Maybe even murder for hire, along with other assorted felonies.

Without the evidence that Dr. Sheridan could have possibly given them, Raleigh was in a wait-and-see mode. There was a lot riding on those banking records because even if Yvette was guilty, Thea doubted the woman would just confess to the growing list of crimes.

It was also possible they'd get something from the crime lab. But they, too, had a mountain of stuff to process. Not just any possible evidence they'd gathered from Sonya and the woods where her body had been found, but also the baby's clothes and carrier. And now the SUV might turn up something, too.

Unless…

"What if Dr. Sheridan was the gunman who shot at us from the SUV?" she asked. It was a question that had been going through her head, along with all those other thoughts, and she was certain that Raleigh had considered it, too.

"I'm sure your boss will have the body tested for gunshot residue," he said, and he didn't add as much venom to the word *boss* as he probably could have, considering that her boss, Egan, was also his half brother. "If Sheridan has GSR on him, then we'll know he fired a gun."

True, but it wouldn't necessarily prove he was the one who'd tried to kill them. Someone could have set up the doctor.

"I can call Egan if you like," she offered.

Raleigh paused as if considering that, but he certainly didn't decline. That's because finding the killer was far more important than their family troubles. "Yeah, if I haven't heard from him by morning."

"If Egan has anything, he'll call," she assured him. "He's a cop through and through like you."

Raleigh opened his mouth, maybe to say he was nothing like Egan, but then he stopped and dragged in a long breath. "I talked to him earlier when you were in the bathroom at the sheriff's office." He paused and gave her a flat look. "He told me to make sure that you were okay."

Thea groaned. Good grief. That was almost identical to what her brother had told Raleigh. "They forget that I'm a cop with just as much training as they have." Well, almost as much.

"No, they remember that. They care about you and are worried because I haven't been able to ID the killer."

She hated that Raleigh was putting all of this on his shoulders. "If I'm the target, then I'm the one responsible for this. I'm the one who dragged you and all of your deputies into the path of a killer."

A possibility that ate away at her as much as Sonya's death. Thea prayed she wasn't the reason for that, too.

The one saving grace in all of this was that the baby was safe. Griff had let them know that when they'd arrived at the safe house, and there'd been no incidents along the way. Now they needed to make sure there wasn't a second baby out there who needed to be rescued from the monsters who'd taken her.

"You should try to get some rest," Raleigh said, pulling her out of her thoughts. "You remember where the guest room is?"

Thea nodded. She remembered though she'd never actually been in it. Whenever she'd stayed over, she'd always been in Raleigh's bed. With both of them naked.

Probably best not to remember that now though.

"I'll need to get back to the office by seven," Raleigh added, already heading in the direction of his bedroom. But he stopped when his phone rang.

Thea didn't groan, but considering the late hour, she figured this was probably bad news. Still, she hoped it was merely an update on the investigation.

"It's Miguel," Raleigh mumbled when he looked at the screen. He hit the answer button and put the call on speaker. It didn't take long for Thea to hear his deputy's voice.

"A detective from San Antonio PD just called," Miguel said. "A woman, Madison Travers, just walked in and confessed to botching the in vitro procedure done on Sonya. And this woman says she believes she knows who tried to kill you."

Chapter Seven

Raleigh wished he'd managed to get a little more sleep. Two hours didn't seem nearly enough, considering the hellish day he was about to face. Still, he was glad he'd managed to get any sleep at all since he'd spent a good deal of the night on the phone with SAPD and his deputies.

Unfortunately, he'd spent some of the night thinking about Thea, too.

He cursed himself for that. He didn't have the time or mental energy to rehash the past, but that's exactly what he'd done anyway.

Having Thea under the same roof with him

was a bad reminder of when they'd been lovers. Worse, Raleigh was certain it was the same for her. He hadn't missed the heated looks she'd given him. Also hadn't missed her expression that told him she was just as frustrated as he was about this.

He forced his attention back where it belonged—on the drive to the sheriff's office. No one was following Thea and him, but he needed to make sure it stayed that way. He needed to get to work in one piece so he could question Madison Travers. At least that was one of the things he had to do.

But at the moment the woman was his top priority.

She had not only confessed to the in vitro snafu but also claimed to know who wanted to kill them. Unfortunately, she hadn't wanted to share that info with the San Antonio cops but had insisted instead on talking to Raleigh.

He very much wanted to talk to Madison, too, but Raleigh hoped this wasn't some kind of ruse to get at Thea and him again. That's why he hadn't taken Thea to San Antonio to question the woman. Instead, SAPD had waited until morning to bring Madison to Durango Ridge, and she was now waiting for them in an interview room.

Thea was keeping watch as well, even though she was on the phone with Egan to get an update on the Dr. Sheridan murder investigation. She hadn't put the call on speaker, maybe because she hadn't wanted to emphasize to her boss that she was in a cruiser with his illegitimate half brother. But judging from the way her forehead was bunched up, she didn't like what she was hearing from Egan.

"A problem?" Raleigh asked as soon as she'd finished the call.

"No. But it wasn't the answers we wanted."

Hell. As much as he disliked the idea of having his half brother connected to this case, Raleigh had hoped that Egan would be able to clear up some things. Raleigh would take all the help he could get.

"There was gunshot residue on Dr. Sheridan's jacket but not his hands," Thea continued a moment later. "Egan thinks the pattern indicates that it was transferred from the actual shooter to the doctor."

And that meant someone had tried to make it look as if Sheridan had killed himself in the SUV. If the doctor had actually done that, then the GSR should have been on his hands.

"So he was murdered," Raleigh concluded.

Thea nodded. "Egan said the placement of the gun was wrong, too. Sheridan was left-handed, and the gun was in his right."

So they were dealing with a sloppy killer. Or one that had panicked.

"There's more," she went on. "One of Sheridan's neighbors saw him yesterday afternoon with two men that she didn't recognize. She said she didn't think anything of it at the time, but after she heard about his death, she called SAPD. She didn't see a gun or anything, but she thought the men looked menacing."

"Did she give the cops a description of the men?" he asked.

Another nod just as her phone dinged with a message. "They're having her work with a sketch artist, too, so we might have something we can put out to the media."

That was a long shot, but it was all he had right now.

"There was a picture on Sheridan's phone," Thea went on when he pulled to a stop in front of the sheriff's office. "Egan just texted it to me. It's the same photo that the kidnappers sent Nick."

She showed him the photo on the screen, and it was indeed a match. But what did it mean? Had Sheridan been involved with the second kidnapping? Or had it all been a hoax? Raleigh was thinking hoax since the kidnapper still hadn't called back. Although if Sheridan was the kidnapper, that would explain why Nick had never gotten a call back.

"I'm hoping one of your deputies made lots of coffee," Thea grumbled as they hurried inside.

Raleigh was hoping the same thing, though it was asking a lot of mere caffeine to get rid of the headache he already had. The headache got worse when he immediately saw Nick and Yvette coming toward them. There was a guy in a suit behind Yvette. Her lawyer, no doubt, and he cut ahead of the pair. He didn't stop until he was practically right in Raleigh's face.

"You either need to charge my client or let

her go," the man insisted. According to the business card he handed Raleigh, his name was Vernon Cutler. And yeah, he was a lawyer all right.

Raleigh was just ornery enough to say he was charging her, but he looked at Dalton to see if anything had come back on the bank records or the safe-deposit box.

Dalton shook his head. "If Mrs. O'Hara paid off hired guns, she didn't use those bank accounts, and there was nothing missing from the safe-deposit box. Mr. O'Hara gave us a list of the contents, and everything was there."

"What about any activity on Yvette's cell phone?" Raleigh pressed. He'd asked his deputies to check that to see if there were any irregularities.

"She made eight calls to Sonya yesterday. Two before the body was discovered and the rest came after."

"I call Sonya every day," Yvette argued. *"Called,"* she corrected, her voice cracking. "When she didn't answer, I kept trying to reach her because I was worried about her."

Raleigh heard every word of that, but it wasn't those calls that interested him. "Did she have any new contacts over the past week or so?" he pressed.

"No," Dalton answered. "Every call on her phone checked out."

That didn't mean the woman hadn't used a disposable cell phone, or a burner as it was called, but if she had, there was no proof.

"We got the search warrant for the O'Haras' house," Dalton explained. "Miguel's on the way there now to go through it with SAPD."

Good. But a search like that could take hours, and Raleigh doubted they'd find a murder weapon or anything else incriminating that Yvette had just happened to leave lying around.

So basically the only thing Raleigh had against the woman was the recorded argument that she'd had with Sonya. A recording that likely wouldn't be admissible in court since Sonya hadn't informed Yvette that the conversation was being recorded. Of course, the obstruction of justice charge was still on the table, but Raleigh had other more immediate issues.

Madison Travers, for one.

And there was his mother. He saw Alma in his office with her lawyer and longtime friend, Simon Lindley. Neither looked especially happy, and Simon was likely going to pitch a fit that Raleigh was questioning Alma.

"Your client is free to go," Raleigh told Vernon Cutler. "For now," he tacked on to that.

"But I don't want to go," Yvette said. "I want to stay here in case the kidnapper calls."

"You'll have to wait elsewhere," Raleigh told her. "This place is getting pretty crowded."

"Come on," Yvette's lawyer insisted, but he had to practically drag the woman out of the building.

"You should probably try to get some rest, too," Raleigh told Nick. No way though would he force the man to go.

"I managed a nap in the break room. I'd like to stay just in case."

Raleigh nodded and was about to make his way to the coffeepot, but then he saw Thea coming toward him with two cups of coffee in her hand. She was already sipping one and handed the other to him. He thanked her and downed as much of it as he could, even though it was scalding hot. Thea seemed to be doing the same thing.

"Thanks," he said to Thea, and he glanced at his mom. She wasn't glaring. Alma had a sad, how-could-you-do-this-to-me expression on her face. It was very effective at making Raleigh feel like a jerk and a bad son. But since he was a son with a badge, he had no choice about bringing her in.

"I didn't know about the search warrant," Nick said.

Since Nick had been cooperative so far, Raleigh hadn't expected to hear or see any hesitation, but he sure as heck saw it now. "Why? Is that a problem?"

Nick didn't jump to answer that. "No." But that didn't sound like the truth. And it was something Raleigh would need to dig a little deeper into once he dealt with the other issues. However, he kept his eyes on Nick as he headed back down the hall. The man also took out his phone and made a call.

"You think he doesn't want us to find something in his house?" Thea asked. She'd obviously picked up on the bad vibe, too.

"Maybe." And maybe the guy was just acting punchy because he was exhausted. Something that Raleigh totally understood.

"I'll have Dalton do the interview with my mother," Raleigh explained to Thea, "but I need to speak to her first. You don't have to be part of that unless you're a glutton for punishment."

"Consider me a glutton." She gave him a half smile, but then she quickly got serious again. "I want to hear what anyone has to say about what's gone on. We need to catch Sonya's killer."

Yeah, they did, but he wished he'd had more sleep and more coffee before dealing with this. His mom was only half the problem. She was usually civil, even when Raleigh was calling her into question, but Simon could be a protective SOB. Part of Raleigh was pleased that Simon was so protective, but sometimes that got in the way.

Raleigh was certain it would now, too.

"Why are you doing this?" Simon snapped the moment Raleigh went into his office.

He looked Simon straight in the eyes. "Because a woman was murdered and a baby was kidnapped. A second baby might be missing, as well. I'm sure my mother would want to help with that in any way she could."

"I would." Alma got to her feet, and he saw the concern in her eyes. "Are the babies all right?"

"One of them is. She's with social services. I'm not sure about the other. That's what I'm trying to find out." Along with learning if the still-kidnapped baby even existed.

"I'll help any way I can," his mother said,

and then she looked past him and at Thea. They'd met when Thea and he had been dating and while his mom had still been with Warren, and his mother had been friendly to Thea then.

Not so much now though.

Alma didn't glare at Thea or anything, but she quickly turned back to Raleigh, putting her attention solely on him. "You think I know something that could help with this case?" Alma asked.

Simon huffed. "You're a person of interest, Alma. Because Sonya worked for you, and you fired her."

This was the first Raleigh was hearing about the firing, so he stared at his mother, waiting for her to fill him in.

"You really don't think I'd kill Sonya because of what went on two years ago?" His mother patted her chest as if to steady her heart.

Raleigh answered that with a question of his own. "Why'd you fire her?"

"Because she stole some money from Alma, that's why," Simon barked.

"Because she *might* have stolen it," Alma corrected. "Some money went missing. And no, I didn't feel the need to tell you. I handled it myself."

"She didn't tell you because you would have arrested Sonya," Simon interrupted. "Especially if you'd heard the way Sonya talked to your mother. She yelled at her."

Sonya did have a temper, but he hadn't known about her being a possible thief. He hoped that was the extent of the woman's criminal behavior. He definitely didn't want her connected to the mix-up at the fertility clinic, but that was something he could ask Madison Travers.

"Sonya yelled at you?" Thea repeated.

His mother nodded, but Raleigh saw Simon's eyes narrow. "Oh, no. You're not going to pin Sonya's murder on Alma."

Maybe not, but Simon had just provided a motive for his mother to be part of this. It wasn't a strong motive, but it wasn't one he could just overlook, either.

"Did you bring him here?" Simon snapped.

It took Raleigh a moment to realize that Simon was looking over his shoulder. And his attention was on the man who'd just walked into the squad room.

Warren.

Hell.

"I need another cup of coffee for this," Raleigh grumbled, and he turned around to face the man. "It's not a good time," he warned Warren.

Warren acknowledged that with a nod. "I just wanted to check on Thea. And you."

Raleigh hadn't wanted to be included in that, though Warren's concern did seem genuine. As genuine as his mother's hurt and Simon's anger. Raleigh's anger, too.

"Come on, Alma." Simon took her by the arm. "We're leaving."

Alma didn't put up a fuss about that, but Raleigh had to. "You can take her to the interview room, but you can't leave. Not just yet. I need you to give Dalton your statement about the time Sonya worked for you," he added to his mother.

"She can do that another time, when he's not here," Simon spat out, his venom obviously aimed at Warren.

"I'll go," Warren said.

"No." Alma spoke up. "Simon and I can go to the interview room." She aimed a sharp look at Simon. "Let's just get this done."

Raleigh was glad that his mom had stood up to Simon. It was something she had to do often since Simon always seemed to be trying to control her. Not just in legal situations but in the rest of her life, too.

"Thanks," Raleigh told his mom. He didn't say anything to Simon, but the man glared at Thea, Warren and him on the way out of the office and all the way to the interview room.

"I didn't mean to cause trouble," Warren said. "I was just worried about Thea." He had his hands crammed in his pockets, but he looked as if he wanted to hug her.

"I'm all right," Thea assured him. "I'll be back in McCall Canyon soon, but Raleigh and I need to work this case."

Warren nodded and took out his phone from

his pocket. "I've been studying it, too, and I know you probably don't want my help," he added to Raleigh, "but I might have found something."

Warren showed them the photos on his phone. Photos that Raleigh knew well because they were side-by-side shots of the two scrawled warnings that had been left at the scenes of Hannah's and Sonya's murders.

"Egan got the second photo of Sonya's wall from the lab," Warren explained. "He showed it to me since I'm still working to solve Hannah's case."

"*Unofficially* working," Raleigh automatically snapped, but then he waved that off.

He didn't like Warren, but if he'd been a retired cop with an unsolved murder, he would have kept at it, as well. Especially if he'd known the victim the way that Warren had known Hannah. This was personal for Warren, and Raleigh couldn't fault the man for putting his heart into the investigation.

"I have a friend who's a handwriting expert," Warren went on, "and I had him compare the two messages. As you know, it's hard to do a handwriting analysis on something like this, but he believes it's a match, that the same person wrote both messages."

Raleigh had another look at the photos and the warning. *This is for Sheriff Warren McCall.* They certainly looked the same.

"The killer could have used the same hired thug for both," Raleigh pointed out. "It wouldn't have been Marco though since he was in jail a year ago."

Warren made a sound of agreement. "But what if the killer himself wrote these? If this is someone with a grudge this big against me, maybe he or she wanted to do it himself?"

Raleigh nearly snapped at the addition of

"she" because it referred to his mother. And while Raleigh couldn't see Alma killing two women, maybe someone close to her had.

Someone like Simon.

"I'll make sure Dalton asks Simon his whereabouts for both murders," Raleigh assured Warren.

"You really think Simon could be a killer?" Thea asked.

Raleigh lifted his shoulder. "I think he loves my mother enough to do pretty much anything. He was questioned about your shooting," he added to Warren. And even though Simon's name had been cleared, at the time he had been at the top of Raleigh's suspect list.

Warren certainly knew that because he'd probably studied every aspect of that investigation. "I… We," he amended, "need to get Hannah's killer so we can try to locate her missing child. The baby would be a year old now, and the biological parents need answers. *I* need answers. Maybe I'll get them if you can find who murdered Sonya."

Raleigh intended to do everything possible to make sure the killer was caught. "Sonya's murder could have been a copycat," he reminded Warren. "If so, then the person who left that message on her wall could have studied the one on Hannah's and made sure the signatures were similar."

"Yes," Warren readily admitted. "And if so, then I've wasted your time. Either way, catch this SOB."

Warren brushed his hand along Thea's arm, and then he headed out, leaving Raleigh with a boatload of feelings that he didn't want. He definitely didn't want to feel anything but disgust for this married man who'd carried on a secret affair with his mother.

Thea shut the door after Warren left. "Are

you okay?" she asked. Since that simple question could cover a lot of territory, Raleigh just waited for her to add more. "I know it can't be easy for you to be around Warren."

"It's not." And that was all he intended to say about it.

But it apparently wasn't all that Thea intended to do. She slipped her arm around him and eased him to her. "Yes, I know this isn't smart, but if anyone needs a hug right now, it's you."

The cowboy in him wouldn't admit that, but the hug did feel, well, good. Comforting, even. At least it did for a couple of seconds, and then it turned to something else when that brainless part of him behind the zipper of his jeans reminded him that this was Thea.

And that he still wanted her.

He pulled back, intending to step away, but he made the mistake of looking down at her. Oh, man. It felt as if the air had caught fire. Something was certainly blazing, and he made the mistake even worse by leaning in and brushing his mouth over hers.

That sure didn't help cool the heat any.

And even though he realized that it wasn't helping, he didn't stop. He would have just stood there and kept on kissing her until things went well beyond the comforting-hug stage. Thankfully though, Thea seemed to still have some common sense because she's the one who moved away from him.

"I was right," she said, her voice silky and filled with breath. "That wasn't smart."

Yeah, but it was good. Which, of course, made it bad. Especially bad because he had other things he should be doing. Things that could end up keeping Thea out of the path of a killer.

"I need to talk to Madison Travers," Raleigh grumbled.

He didn't wait around, partly because he didn't want to talk about the kiss that shouldn't have happened and also because he was anxious to see if the woman had any information they could use. Thea followed him, of course, but he wanted her to hear this just in case she picked up on something he might miss. After all, she knew more about the fertility clinic than he did, since she'd been investigating it for a year.

Madison Travers was waiting for them in the interview room, and she immediately got to her feet. She was petite, right at five-feet tall, and she immediately made nervous glances at both Thea and him.

She didn't have a lawyer with her, but there was a uniformed cop at the table. He'd obviously escorted Madison there from SAPD headquarters, and he introduced himself as Dewayne Rodriquez.

"I've read Ms. Travers her rights," Officer Rodriquez said. "And she waived her right to an attorney."

"Because I don't need a lawyer to tell the truth," Madison blurted out. Judging from her red eyes and puffy face, she'd been crying.

Raleigh could have argued that she might indeed need an attorney because if she had done something illegal, then she could be arrested.

"You're Sheriff Lawton?" Madison asked.

He nodded and tipped his head to Thea. "And this is Deputy Morris from the McCall Canyon Sheriff's office. I understand you're responsible for the botched in vitro procedure for Sonya Burney?" Raleigh started. Both Thea and he took a seat at the table, and Madison sat across from them. "I want to hear all about that, but I'm especially interested in who tried to kill us and how you came by that information."

Madison seemed to lose even more color in her already pale face, but then Raleigh had made sure he sounded like a tough lawman. He wasn't going to let the woman skate just because she'd voluntarily gone to the cops. That's because she hadn't come clean for nearly nine months.

"Yes, I'm the one who messed up Sonya's in vitro. I misplaced Mrs. O'Hara's eggs. At least I guess I did because I couldn't find them when we got ready to do the procedure. I told Dr. Bryce Sheridan, and he said he'd take care of it."

"Dr. Sheridan?" Raleigh questioned. "So he knew about this?"

"Of course," Madison answered without hesitating. "He did an insemination instead.

That means he just used Mr. O'Hara's semen to inject into Sonya, not the fertilized eggs as originally planned." She paused. "We didn't think it would be successful. Usually it isn't. So we thought we'd have time to find Mrs. O'Hara's eggs before we did the real in vitro in a couple of months."

"Why didn't you just come clean with Sonya and the O'Haras?" Thea asked, taking the question right out of Raleigh's mouth.

Now she hesitated. "I'd already gotten in trouble for improperly storing another sample, and I would have been fired. Bryce was covering for me." Madison started crying again when she said the doctor's name. *Bryce.* "Plus, the clinic is being sued by a former client who's claiming we illegally released medical information about her to her ex-husband. We couldn't have handled another lawsuit. It would have closed us down."

From everything Raleigh was hearing, closing them down wouldn't be a bad thing. Two errors made by Madison and a lawsuit weren't a stellar track record.

"You and Dr. Sheridan were lovers?" Raleigh pressed.

She nodded, wiped away her tears, but kept sobbing. "And now he's dead. Murdered. That's the reason I went to the cops. I thought somebody might try to kill me, too. Those men did this to him, didn't they?"

"Men?" Thea and Raleigh said in unison.

Madison grabbed some tissues from a box on the table, nodding while she blew her nose. "Two of them. They were wearing suits and had badges. They came to the clinic and asked to speak to Bryce. I told them it was his day off, and then they said they wanted to know the names of all his current patients."

Well, that was interesting. "Were the men cops?"

Madison shook her head. "They said they were FBI. But after they left, I got to thinking that there was something suspicious about them. I mean, they should have known I couldn't just give them the names without a court order."

"The FBI didn't send anyone to the clinic," Officer Rodriquez verified.

So the guys were posing as law enforcement. "When was this?" Raleigh asked Madison.

"About a week ago."

Raleigh figured that was plenty of time for someone who'd planned on attacking Sonya. "Describe the men."

Madison wiped her eyes again while she continued. "I only got a good look at one of them. The other stayed in the waiting room, and he had on a hat and dark glasses. But the other one, the one who talked to me, was bald. Oh, and he had a tattoo on his neck, but he'd tried to cover it up with makeup. I could see the makeup on the collar of his shirt."

Raleigh texted Dalton to bring him a picture of Marco, but he continued with the questions while he waited. "Does the clinic have security cameras?"

"Not inside the building, but we have one in the parking lot."

Raleigh looked at Officer Rodriquez again. "We asked the security company who monitors the camera to provide us with footage," the cop answered. "But they're stalling because they say it could violate patients' rights to release it. We're working on a court order, but it could take a while if they keep fighting it—especially since the murder didn't take place on the grounds or inside the clinic."

Well, hell. That complicated things. "Would

it do any good if I talked to them?" Raleigh asked.

Officer Rodriquez lifted his shoulder. "It wouldn't hurt. Their office is in San Antonio. Maybe you could show them a picture of the murdered patient so they can see that the footage is part of an active murder investigation."

Raleigh looked at Thea, and she nodded. "We need that footage."

He couldn't argue with her about that, but he was worried about the risks of being out in the open with Thea. Still, this was the best shot they had right now. Well, unless he could convince SAPD to put more pressure on the security company.

There was a knock at the door, and a moment later Dalton came in with Marco's mug shot. When Raleigh turned the screen in Madison's direction, the woman shook her head.

"Who is he?" Madison demanded, the fear in her voice. "Is he the one who killed Bryce?"

No, he'd been dead by then, but Marco had certainly been willing to murder Thea.

"Is this one of the men who visited you at the clinic?" Raleigh asked.

"No. I've never seen that guy. Why would you think he was there?"

Raleigh was hoping Marco had been there so it would tie everything up, linking Marco to both Sonya's attack and the clinic. He needed to find out if Dr. Sheridan had been murdered because the killers/kidnappers thought he was onto them. If so, they might consider Madison a loose end, too.

And of course, Thea also fell into that same loose-end category.

But Madison had admitted she hadn't gotten a good look at the man with the hat who'd stayed in the waiting room, so maybe that one had been Marco.

"Sonya knew the child she was carrying

was hers," Thea said to Madison. "Did you tell her?"

Again, Madison took her time answering. "Yes. I called her yesterday and then sent her results of the amnio to prove it. I just couldn't stay quiet after I got that visit from Nick O'Hara."

Even Officer Rodriquez seemed surprised by that. "When did Nick visit you?" Raleigh pressed.

"Two days ago." Madison's voice cracked. "He had a meeting with Bryce, and I didn't mean to overhear what they said, but Mr. O'Hara was talking pretty loud. He told Bryce that he was leaving his wife, Yvette."

Raleigh had thought that might happen. He certainly hadn't seen a lot of affection between Yvette and Nick. But something about this didn't make sense.

"Why would Nick go to Dr. Sheridan with this?" Raleigh asked.

"He wanted to see the surrogacy agreement. He said he couldn't find his copy but that he thought he remembered there being a way out of the arrangement. Mr. O'Hara didn't want to share custody with his wife. He wanted full custody for himself."

That didn't mesh with what Yvette had told them. She'd claimed that Nick was having second thoughts about the baby, but maybe he was just having second thoughts about having a baby with her.

"After I heard Mr. O'Hara say that," Madison went on, "I knew I had to tell Sonya the truth, so I called her."

"What phone did you use to do that?" Thea immediately asked.

"The one in my office."

Raleigh jumped right on that. "The office where those two men visited you?" He waited for Madison to confirm that with a nod. "Were you with the two men the whole time they were there?"

"No. I went up the hall to see if I could find our other doctor to talk to them, but he was with a patient." Madison's eyes widened. "Do you think they planted a bug or something?"

Yes, he did. Apparently so did Officer Rodriquez because he called someone to ask them to search the clinic for an eavesdropping device.

"Oh, God," Madison blurted out. "If they heard that, then they heard me say I was suspicious of them. They heard everything I said to Sonya."

Raleigh leaned in closer. "What exactly did you say to Sonya?"

The tears started up again. "I told her what I did about the botched procedure, and she was upset. She said that she was going to call you and that you would probably help her go someplace else to have the baby. A place where she could think about what she was going to do. I liked Sonya, and she said she trusted you. That's why I insisted on talking to you."

So, if Sonya was thinking about leaving town, that might have prompted her killer to spring into action. But it still didn't tell Raleigh who'd murdered her.

Sonya had told Yvette. They had the recording to prove that. But Raleigh wasn't sure if Sonya had had time to phone Nick or not. If she had, the man certainly hadn't mentioned it.

There was another knock at the door. His other deputy Alice this time. She was holding a tablet, and Raleigh could tell from her expression that she had something important to tell him.

"Excuse me for a moment," Raleigh said to Officer Rodriquez and Madison, and both Thea and he went out into the hall with his deputy.

"The lab called," Alice explained, "and they found a fingerprint on the bottom of the carrier seat that the baby was in when you found her." She glanced at the notes on her tablet. "They got a match on the print. A guy name Buck Tanner. He's a career criminal, and that's why his prints were in the system."

Raleigh felt some of the pressure leave his chest. They finally had a name, which meant they could locate this snake and bring him in.

"Is Buck a bald guy with a neck tattoo?" Thea asked.

Alice nodded and pulled up a picture of him. He matched Madison's description of one of her visitors, and Raleigh was about to take the photo in to have her confirm it when Alice stopped him.

"There's more," Alice went on. "I found the name of Buck's lawyer for his last two arrests. It was Simon."

Chapter Eight

Thea knew Raleigh was on edge about this decision to go to Shaw's Security Company in San Antonio to try to get the camera footage from the fertility clinic. She was on edge about it, too, but this was the fastest way they had of finding out who'd visited the clinic with Buck Tanner.

If it was his lawyer, Simon, then Raleigh would be able to make an arrest.

Of course, that alone wouldn't be enough to convict Simon of Sonya's murder. Simon could always claim that he went to the clinic with his client, maybe to discuss something totally unrelated to Sonya. Simon could even dispute what Madison had said. After all, Madison had botched the in vitro procedure and then lied about it. She wasn't exactly a credible witness.

It would have helped if Sonya had recorded her chat with Madison, but if she had done that, it wasn't with the other recordings. In fact, the only conversations that Sonya had taped were with Yvette, and that hadn't started until six weeks into Sonya's pregnancy.

Why?

Maybe Sonya hadn't trusted the woman. But that only brought Thea back to another *why.*

Even though the questions were important, Thea made sure she kept watch around them while Alice drove Raleigh and her to San Antonio. It wasn't a long trip—less than an hour—but they'd taken precautions. They were in the bullet-resistant cruiser, and Alice could give them backup. Raleigh had even considered sending just Alice and Dalton, but he had decided he, as the sheriff, stood a better chance of talking the security company owner into letting him view the footage. Thea agreed.

The visit was a risk, and it also ate up a good chunk of the morning, but Raleigh and she weren't being idle. Thea was reading through the report that the lab had sent them on the evidence that had been processed, and Raleigh was on the phone with his deputy Miguel.

"No, don't ask Simon anything about the visit to the fertility clinic," Raleigh said to Miguel. The call wasn't on speaker, but since Raleigh and she were side by side, Thea could still hear bits and pieces of the conversation. "Just keep looking for Buck Tanner and any financial links between him and Simon. Links that can't be explained as payment for Simon's legal services."

Raleigh and she had already started looking for Buck before they left Durango Ridge, but the man wasn't answering his phone, nor had he been at his house when SAPD had sent an officer out to bring him in for questioning. If Buck was responsible for the murders and the attack, then he had probably gone into hiding.

"Madison's in protective custody," Raleigh relayed to her as soon as he finished his call with Miguel. "She went willingly because she's convinced she could be a target."

She could be. Ditto for Raleigh and her. And Warren. Since Warren seemed to be at the center of the two dead surrogates, he was perhaps in danger, but unlike Madison, he'd refused any kind of protection. Thea only hoped that Egan and his brother, Court, would keep an eye on him. At least Rachel and the baby were safe, and Thea wanted to make sure it stayed that way.

"What about Nick?" she asked. "Was Miguel able to get in touch with him to ask about the meeting he had with Dr. Sheridan?"

Raleigh shook his head and made a sound of frustration. "He's not answering his phone, either. Someone's on the way to check on him."

Good. Because of all the bad stuff that'd gone on, it was possible that Nick was in danger, too. Besides, it was odd that the man wasn't answering his phone, because he'd seemed so anxious for a call from the kidnapper. Maybe though he'd given up hope about them calling back.

"I don't suppose there have been any reports of missing babies similar to the one in the picture that the kidnappers sent him?" Thea continued.

Another headshake. "But we still don't know

how old the picture is. Or where it was taken. It could be a photo of a baby that was taken off the internet."

True. The baby in the photo might not even be missing, much less kidnapped and being held for ransom. They'd done an image search on the internet to find possible matches, but that hadn't turned up anything, either.

Raleigh tipped his head to the report Thea had been reading. "Anything new in that lab report?"

"Not really new, but Buck's print wasn't from a single finger. It was actually a hand-print, and it was in the right position for some-one who was maybe holding the baby carrier to keep it steady. In other words, the print wasn't planted."

Not that Thea thought it had been, but it would be nice to rule it out if that's what Buck claimed had happened.

"I also brought these," she said, taking the hard copy photos from the file. They were pictures of Simon, Marco, Nick and even Yvette. "I wanted to see if anyone from the security company recognized them. That way, if they don't let us view the footage, then maybe they'll look at it and compare it to the photos."

Raleigh made another sound of approval, though she was sure he preferred to review the footage himself.

His phone dinged with a text, and he frowned when he read it and showed her the screen. It was from Dalton.

SAPD found an eavesdropping device in Madison's office.

Thea groaned. "That means the visitors— and perhaps the killer, too—knew that Madison had told Sonya about the botched in vitro." She paused, giving that some thought. "You think that was the trigger that caused the kidnapper/killer to go after Sonya?"

He paused, too. "Maybe. And if so, then it points to Yvette as being the killer."

"Yes, it does. Once we're back in Durango Ridge, we need to bring the woman back in for questioning."

Thea saw the sudden change in Raleigh's eyes, and it didn't take her long to figure out why. It was the "we" in that comment. It made it sound as if they were a team. Which they were. But that didn't mean he was comfortable with it.

"About that kiss," he said a moment later. He kept his voice low, probably so that Alice wouldn't hear. "It really shouldn't have happened."

"I won't argue with that." But for some stupid reason, Thea found herself fighting back a smile. There was nothing to smile about, even though the kiss had been pretty amazing. Of course, every kiss she'd ever had with Raleigh fell into that category.

"It's not just because we're working this case," he went on. "It's the baggage."

No need for him to remind her of that. "Because of Warren. Any kiss between us involves him, too."

Raleigh's eyebrow came up. "Trust me. I wasn't thinking about Warren during that."

She lost her fight with the smile, causing Raleigh to add some profanity under his breath. "Neither was I."

Thea would have liked to have promised that there wouldn't be another kiss, but she wasn't in the habit of lying to herself. If Raleigh and she were thrown together, they'd likely kiss again. And perhaps even do more. That was the reason she shouldn't stay at his house another night. The fatigue and adrenaline were already sky-high and that could bring down their already low defenses even more.

Best not to complicate things by having sex with Raleigh. Even if that was something that sounded darn good to her.

She was about to tell him that she would call Court or one of her other fellow deputies to escort her home tonight and stay with her, but Alice took the turn into the parking lot of the security company. That conversation would have to wait.

As Thea had been doing the whole time they'd been on the road, she glanced around, looking for any signs of trouble. It wasn't a large building at all, and there were only two vehicles in the parking lot.

Raleigh had given the owner, Dan Shaw, a heads-up call that they were on the way to see him, and she hoped that one of the two cars belonged to Shaw. Thea didn't want him stalling them by ducking out on this visit.

Alice didn't park in any of the spots. Instead, she pulled directly in front of the door. "You want me to go in with you?" Alice asked Raleigh.

"No. Wait here and make sure no one else comes inside."

Thea hadn't needed a reminder of the possible danger that came with a visit like this, but that caused her heartbeat to kick up a significant notch. She didn't draw her gun, but she kept her hand in position as Raleigh and she got out and hurried inside.

There was a reception desk just a couple of yards from the door, but there was no one seated at it. In fact, there was no one in the room. Despite that, nothing seemed out of order. There was a cup of coffee and a sandwich still in its plastic wrapper next to an open laptop on the desk.

"Mr. Shaw?" Raleigh called out.

Nothing. But Thea didn't go into alarm mode just yet. There was an office to the right, just off the reception area, and a hall to the left, where there were several other rooms.

Raleigh shouted the man's name again, and when Shaw didn't answer, Raleigh took out his phone and called him. Almost immediately, Thea heard the ringing sound in one of the back rooms off the hall.

Thea looked up at Raleigh and saw that he was just as concerned as she was. Maybe this was just a case of the man trying to hide from them, but it could be something much worse.

Raleigh and Thea drew their guns.

They started toward the hall, but she heard another sound in the room across from the reception desk. Someone was in there, and it sounded as if the person moaned.

Raleigh put his phone away and positioned himself in front of her. "Watch our backs," he told her.

Thea would because, after all, the owner's phone was on the other end of the building. Maybe the owner, too. But it was suspicious that he hadn't come out when Raleigh had called out for him. Suspicious, too, that someone else was nearby in the other room and hadn't said anything.

Raleigh walked closer to the room, keeping his steps slow and cautious, and once he reached the door, he readied his gun.

Then he cursed.

Thea had to lean to the side to see what had caused that reaction, and she soon spotted the woman on the floor. She was on her stomach, her arms and legs flung out in an awkward pose.

And there was blood on her head.

RALEIGH FELT THAT kick of emotion. A mix of dread and adrenaline. There was also some fear, since he figured that Thea and he had just walked into a crime scene.

His gaze slashed to every corner of the room. It was an office with a desk, but there was no one at the desk or beneath it. Only the woman on the floor.

"Is she still alive?" Thea asked, automatically taking out her phone. No doubt to call for an ambulance.

While he continued to keep watch, Raleigh stooped down and put his fingers to the woman's throat. "She's got a pulse." But in addition to what appeared to be blunt-force trauma to the head, she also had two distinctive marks on her neck.

Someone had used a stun gun on her.

Just as they had on Thea when she'd been at Sonya's house.

"Get Alice in here," Raleigh told Thea as she continued to make the call. "I need to check those back rooms where we heard the phone ringing."

And he didn't want to do that unless he had someone to help him protect Thea. Of course, Thea wouldn't appreciate him thinking like that, but she'd already come too close to dying, not once but twice.

Thea nodded and headed for the door but stopped when they heard another sound. Not a moan or a phone ringing this time. Someone was moving around in the room at the end of the hall. There was a sign next to that particular door, and it had Shaw's name on it, which meant that was his office.

"Call Alice and tell her to get in here," Raleigh repeated to Thea. She started to do that, but again the sound interrupted her.

But it was more than an interruption this time.

Shaw's office door flew open, and before Raleigh could even get a glimpse of the person who'd opened it, a shot blasted through the air. The bullet slammed into the wall right next to where Raleigh was standing. Another quarter of an inch, and he'd have been dead.

Raleigh hooked his arm around Thea, dragging her to the floor, but she'd already started in that direction anyway. Good thing, too, because more shots came. Thick, loud blasts that tore apart not just the wall behind them but also the reception desk. Since the desk wasn't much of a barrier at all, Raleigh pulled Thea into the room with the unconscious woman.

The woman moaned as if trying to warn them, but it was too late for that. Thea and he were under fire, and if Raleigh lifted his head to shoot back, he'd be an easy target.

Since the injured woman was too close to the door, Thea dragged her to the side so she wouldn't get hit by a stray bullet, and then Thea hurried back to him. A place he wished she wouldn't be, but he doubted there was any way he could talk her out of it. Plus, he needed the backup.

His phone buzzed, and when Raleigh saw Alice's name on the screen, he handed it to Thea. "Tell her to call SAPD if she hasn't already, but I don't want her coming through that door." She'd be too easy of a target for the shooter.

Thea did as he said, but her attention stayed

in the direction of the gunman. So did Raleigh's. Judging from the angle of the shot, it was just one guy, but he could have brought a buddy with him who was holding Shaw. And Raleigh didn't have to guess what the thugs wanted.

They didn't want Thea and him to see the footage from the security camera.

That told Raleigh plenty about this situation—that he would almost certainly recognize the other man who'd gone to the fertility clinic to try to get a list of Dr. Sheridan's patients.

Maybe it was Nick or Simon.

Of course, it could be someone who could be linked to one of those two. And that's why it was important for Raleigh to get his hands on that footage.

"SAPDs on the way," Thea said when she finished her call to Alice.

Good. Because the angle of the shots changed. This thug was moving closer, no doubt trying to get in position to kill them both. That meant it was time for Raleigh to do something about that.

He stayed down, but he levered himself up just enough to send a bullet in the shooter's direction. Raleigh doubted he'd hit the guy, but it caused the man to growl out some raw curse words, and he kept shooting. However, Raleigh had gotten a decent look at the guy, and he was wearing a ski mask.

Raleigh fired another shot, too, and quickly moved back to cover. Well, as much cover as he had. The bullets were tearing through the wall, and it wouldn't be long before Thea and he couldn't use it for cover.

"Let's shoot at him together," Thea said.

He hated the idea because it would mean her being in the open. For a few seconds anyway. But SAPD or an ambulance wouldn't be able to get in and help until they'd contained the gunman. The woman definitely needed medical attention, and it was possible Shaw did, too.

"Fire now?" Thea asked.

She waited for Raleigh to nod, and together they leaned out, both of them pulling their triggers at the same time. Raleigh braced himself for the guy to shoot back. But he didn't. In fact, there were no gunshots from him, no profanity. Just the sound of someone running.

Hell, now the snake was trying to get away.

Raleigh got up, ready to fire, but the man was already ducking back into the office, and he slammed the door.

"If you want Shaw dead," the man shouted, "then go ahead and try to come back here."

Raleigh didn't want Shaw to die, but he couldn't trust that this goon would just keep him alive. In fact, he might use Shaw as a human shield so he could get out of the building.

The woman on the floor moaned again, a reminder to Raleigh that time wasn't on their side. She could bleed out and die if he didn't do something.

"Stay here with her," he told Thea. Of course, Thea probably didn't mind doing that part, but she knew what this meant.

"You're going out there," she said. Not a question. She knew it had to be done, but he could see the worry all over her face.

Raleigh tried to give her a reassuring nod, but he didn't want to waste another second. With his gun ready, he hurried out of the room, hunkering down behind the reception desk so he could get a better look at the hall. It wasn't long—less that twenty feet—but at any point the thug could open the door and start firing again. If Raleigh couldn't get into one of the other rooms, he'd be a sitting duck.

Even knowing that, he started moving. He ran to the wall right next to the hall and peered around. There was still no sign of the gunman. No sound of him, either. But there was something.

The smell of smoke.

Raleigh got a whiff of it just as it started to seep under and around the sides of the office door. The SOB had set the place on fire.

That gave Raleigh an even greater sense of urgency to do something.

"You might have to get the woman out of here," he called back to Thea, and he prayed that Alice and maybe even SAPD were out there to give her immediate backup.

Raleigh took a deep breath and started running up the hall. The smoke was already getting thicker, and he could smell something burning inside. He put his hand on the door to make sure there'd be no backdraft, but it was still cool to the touch, so he kicked it open.

There were flames all right, and they were already spreading across the wall and ceiling. But that wasn't the only thing that caught Raleigh's attention. It was the back door.

It was wide-open.

And there was no one in the room.

Chapter Nine

Thea sat at Raleigh's desk in the Durango Ridge Sheriff's Office and tried to make sure she didn't show any signs of the raw nerves that were just beneath her skin. She had to be strong. Because Raleigh was already blaming himself enough. If she fell apart, that blame would skyrocket.

No way would he believe this attack wasn't his fault. He was kicking himself for taking her right into the middle of a gunfight. But he'd been in the middle of it, too, and that was one of the main reasons for Thea's raw nerves.

Again, he could have been killed, while trying to protect her.

And now they were in the middle of another round of chaos. One more layer to add to their already complicated investigation. It was more than just a *layer* though to Dan Shaw. He was missing, and his assistant, Sandra Millington, was in the hospital, in critical condition from a cracked skull and blood loss.

Raleigh was pacing in the squad room just outside his office door while he talked to someone in the San Antonio Fire Department. Apparently, he didn't like what he was hearing, which meant she wouldn't like it, either. Still, Thea tried not to focus on what was likely soon-to-be-revealed bad news and instead continued to read Madison's statement.

There wasn't anything new in the statement. At least Thea didn't think there was. But it was hard to concentrate when she could still hear the sound of those gunshots and see the blood on the injured woman.

Mercy.

She prayed Sandra Millington didn't die. There'd already been too many deaths connected to this investigation. Deaths maybe because of her. She couldn't forget that she'd been Marco's target, and that might mean all of this could be happening because of her or something she'd done.

Her phone rang, and Thea was so on edge that she gasped at the unexpected sound. And Raleigh noticed her reaction, too, because it caused his frown to deepen. But Thea wasn't frowning when she saw the name on the screen. Her heart went to her throat.

Because it was Rachel.

"Is the baby all right?" Thea blurted out as soon as she could hit the answer button.

"She's fine. We're all fine," Rachel quickly reassured her. "I was calling to check on you."

It took Thea a moment to get her voice and her breathing back under control. Despite all the horrible things that had happened, it would be a thousand times worse if the baby had been hurt or kidnapped again.

"I'm okay," Thea lied.

Judging from Rachel's huff, she knew it was a lie. "And is Raleigh *okay*?"

"I think so. Neither of us were hurt."

"No, you were just in a burning building with a gunman shooting at you." Rachel mumbled something Thea didn't catch. "I've always worried about Griff, Egan, Court and you. It's a strange feeling to add Raleigh to that worry list."

Thea didn't have any doubts about that. Didn't doubt, either, that Rachel would soon accept Raleigh as her brother. The question was, would Raleigh accept her as his sister? The bitterness he felt for Warren might get in the way of that.

"I do have another reason for calling," Rachel went on. "Griff's been pressuring the lab to get the DNA results on the baby, and we should have those back later today. Depending on what the test says, we have a decision to make. If the baby is Nick and Sonya's biological child, is there a reason for us not to hand over the baby to Nick?"

Thea groaned. Nick was still a person of interest in the attacks, and they certainly hadn't been able to rule him out. "When you have the results, just call Raleigh and me, and we'll go from there."

They might not be able to keep the child out of Nick's custody, but Thea wanted to delay that until they had some answers.

"Will do. Stay safe," Rachel added before she said goodbye.

Thea put her phone away at the same time that Raleigh finished his call with the fire department. He stepped inside the office and shut the door.

"The fire gutted the security company, destroying all the files and computers," he explained. His forehead was still bunched up, and even though he'd stopped pacing, he looked as if he needed to do something to burn off a lot of restless energy. "It's possible that Dan Shaw had files off-site or in an online storage, but we won't know that until we've talked to him or his assistant."

That tightened the muscles in her stomach and chest. Because they might not get a chance to ask either of them. They'd have to find Dan before they could question him, and as much as Thea hated to admit it, he could be dead. Their attacker could have killed him after he'd used Dan to help him escape.

Thea got up from the desk and went closer to Raleigh. "Any news on Sandra Millington?" she asked.

"She's still unconscious and in the ICU, but the hospital will call if there's any change. There's more," Raleigh said after he paused. "Someone torched the fertility clinic, too. No one was hurt," he quickly added. "But since the fire started in the records' room, whatever evidence was there was likely destroyed."

Mercy. No wonder Raleigh had been scowling and frowning when he'd been on the phone with the fire department. This definitely qualified as bad news. However, it did make her wonder...

"What could have been in those records that the killer didn't want us to find?" she asked. "I mean, Madison's already confessed to the botched in vitro, so what else could have been in there?"

"Maybe something to incriminate Yvette or Nick? Exactly what that might be, I'm not sure, and we might never know."

True, and that led her to the call with Rachel. "Rachel said we should have the baby's DNA results today."

Raleigh cursed, which meant she didn't need to fill him in on the rest. "Nick's still not answering his phone. We don't know if that's because he was the person in the security company shooting, if he's a victim or if he's just lying low. Whichever it is, he's not at his house. We know that because SAPD is there now, carrying out a search order, and the only one around is Yvette."

Thea had known about the search order, but she hadn't realized it was already going on. Good. If there was anything incriminating, maybe the cops would find it so they wouldn't have to turn over the baby to Nick. Thea wanted the man to have his child only after he'd been cleared of any suspicion.

Raleigh looked at her, his gaze sliding from her face to her shirt. At first she thought there might be something sexual in that look, but then he cursed. "You have blood on you. Is it yours?"

She looked down at her sleeve and saw the small rip, along with the blood. Thea had noticed it earlier but had forgotten about it. "It's just a scratch." She'd gotten it when one of the gunman's bullets had shattered part of the door frame and had sent some splinters flying right at her.

It might have only been a scratch, but it seemed to be the final straw for Raleigh. He cursed, groaned and scrubbed his hand over his face. He was obviously about to deepen the guilt trip he was already on.

"That's not a good idea," he said when Thea slid her arm around his waist and pulled him to her.

"I know. A lot of what we do isn't a good idea. But going to the security company was," she added.

He eased back enough to look down at her and frown.

"Sandra's alive because we went there," Thea explained. "If we hadn't gotten to her, she could have been unconscious and trapped in that fire."

Raleigh's frown softened just a little. That was the only part of him soft though. His muscles were so tight that it felt as if she was hugging stone.

"The shooter might not have set the fire if we hadn't shown up," Raleigh pointed out, but he groaned again, maybe dismissing that. Because Thea was betting the gunman would indeed have burned down the place just to make sure they didn't get their hands on any evidence.

Since they had dozens of things to do, Thea was a little surprised when Raleigh stayed put. Surprised, too, at the gentle way he used just his fingertips to push her hair from her face. She figured the gentleness was a real effort for him with all that tension in his body.

She got yet another surprise when he leaned in even closer and kissed her. She felt the stubble on his jaw brush over her face. She took in his scent. And his taste.

The kiss packed a punch. A huge one. Maybe it was her frayed nerves, but she found herself leaning right into that kiss. She moved into the rhythm of it until her pulse was thick and throbbing. Until she remembered why she'd gotten involved with Raleigh in the first place.

When he finally pulled back, Thea didn't have to worry that he would see what a wreck she was from the attack. That's because now he was almost certainly seeing the heat in her eyes. Heat that he'd put there from that sizzling kiss.

Raleigh opened his mouth, maybe to apologize, but he didn't get a chance to say anything. That's because they heard Dalton shout out from the squad room.

"Hey, you can't just go in there," Dalton snarled.

But apparently the person thought the deputy's order didn't apply to him because the door flew open, and Simon was there with Dalton right behind him.

"Sorry about this," Dalton said to Raleigh,

and he aimed a cop's glare at Simon. "Some people don't listen."

"*Some people* need to talk to the sheriff," Simon fired back.

But Simon didn't even look at Dalton when he spoke. His attention was on Raleigh and her. Specifically, Simon was noticing the way Thea had her arm around his waist and the fact that their bodies were practically touching. If Simon had come in just seconds earlier, he would have seen more than a touch, but even without that visual, Thea figured the man knew what had gone on.

And he didn't like it.

Maybe because she was close to Warren. However, Simon's anger was directed at Raleigh, too.

"Nice to see you're working so hard to find Sonya's killer," Simon grumbled.

He couldn't have said anything that would

have made Raleigh and her move faster to get away from each other. Because it was true. They shouldn't be kissing when they were in the middle of a murder investigation. And Simon was part of that particular investigation.

"Your deputy called and said you wanted to see me," Simon went on. "Well, I'm a busy man. Busier than you are obviously. So what the heck do you want?"

Raleigh took a moment, maybe to rein in his temper, but he used that time to send a withering glare at Simon. "Where were you at the times of Sonya's and Hannah Neal's murders?"

"What?" Simon howled. And he repeated it. "You think I had something to do with that?"

"I won't know until you've answered the question. It's a simple question, and I'd like an answer—now." There was no sign of a temper in Raleigh's tone, but he was all lawman now.

Dalton must have realized that Raleigh had this under control because he walked away, back toward his desk in the squad room.

"I was at home most of the day when Sonya was killed. And no, I doubt anyone can verify that. I didn't realize at the time that I would need an alibi since I'm not a criminal, and I don't have a criminal record."

Raleigh ignored that mini-tirade and kept on. "What about the day Hannah died? And don't say you don't know who she is, because her murder made front-page news around here."

"That was a year ago," Simon snapped. "No way could I remember something like that off the top of my head."

"Then check your calendar and appointment

book and get back to me. I'd like an answer ASAP."

She hadn't thought Simon's glare could get worse, but it did. "What the hell is this about?"

"Buck Tanner," Raleigh immediately answered.

Thea watched Simon's expression, and she was certain that Raleigh was doing the same. The man's eyes widened for just a fraction of a second, and then his mouth tightened. "My former client. What about him?"

"Former?" Raleigh challenged. "You were his lawyer of record for his last two arrests, one of them only about six months ago."

"We had a parting of the ways. Now, what's this about?" Simon included her in his volleyed glances, though Thea had no intentions of answering him.

"Buck Tanner's prints were on the kidnapped

baby's carrier seat that Thea and I found," Raleigh explained. "I'm guessing you'll insist you don't know anything about that?"

"Of course I don't." But Simon definitely seemed uncomfortable. "Have you talked to him?"

"There's an APB out on him. We'll find him," Raleigh assured him. "Did he have a connection to Sonya? Did he know her?"

"I have no idea." The angry tone was back, but there was still plenty of concern in his eyes. "Are you suggesting that I put him up to something illegal?" Simon didn't wait for an answer. "Because I was his lawyer—that's all."

Raleigh made a *hmm* sound that let Simon know he wasn't exactly buying that. "I'll let you know what Buck says when we find him. And, oh, we're monitoring his phone and bank accounts. Just thought you should know that if you were planning on calling him."

If looks could kill, Simon would have blasted Raleigh and her off the planet. Simon belted out some profanity, turned and stormed out.

"You believe he's innocent?" Thea immediately asked Raleigh.

"I don't know. But something's going on with him."

Thea agreed. Too bad they couldn't find out if that *something* was Simon's plan to get back at Warren. Raleigh must have been thinking the same thing because he took out his phone.

"I'll call my mother and ask her if she ever heard Simon mention Buck," Raleigh explained.

But he didn't get a chance to make the call, because Dalton stepped into the doorway of the office. "SAPD found something when they were searching Yvette and Nick's house. A burner cell that was tucked between the mattresses. They'll send it to the lab to see if they can find out if it was used to make any calls."

"Did Yvette or Nick admit the phone was theirs?" she asked.

Dalton shook his head. "Nick wasn't there, and Yvette left shortly before they found it. You want me to get her in for questioning?"

"Not yet," Raleigh answered. "Wait until we hear back from the lab."

"There's more," Dalton went on. "There was also an envelope underneath a bunch of things in the bottom drawer of the nightstand. The kind of envelope that banks use sometimes when they give you a lot of cash. Someone had marked three thousand dollars on the outside of it, but inside there were only two one-hundred-dollar bills."

Three grand probably wasn't enough to hire two thugs to do your dirty work—like kidnap your surrogate's baby—but maybe it had been some kind of down payment. But the question was, where had Yvette or Nick gotten the money?

Thea looked up at Dalton. "Was there a withdrawal from their bank account in that amount?"

The deputy shook his head. "No cash withdrawal over two-hundred dollars."

It was possible that one of them had made the smaller withdrawals and stashed the money away in those increments, but it would have taken a while for that amount to accumulate. Still, it was doable.

"The lab is going to check for prints on the money," Dalton added.

Good. Then they would know if Nick or Yvette had put it there. Or maybe they both had. This could be their emergency fund, along with the cell phone. Maybe there was no criminal intent whatsoever.

"Let me know what the lab says," Raleigh

reminded Dalton. "And make sure someone is keeping a close watch for Buck."

Dalton nodded. "His cell phone isn't in a service area, but if he gets or receives any calls, we'll know about it."

Since Buck was a career criminal, he'd probably ditched the cell. Too bad there wasn't a way for them to legally monitor Simon's phone, but they would need a court order for that. One they wouldn't be able to get because there wasn't enough evidence against him.

Dalton went back to his desk, leaving Raleigh and her standing there in the suddenly awkward silence. "I need to talk to my mom," he finally said. "Not just to ask her about Buck but because Simon will tell her that he saw you in my arms."

Sweet heaven. With everything else going on, Thea hadn't even considered that. But yes, Simon would tell her, and she didn't have to guess how Alma would handle the news be-cause there was no way Raleigh's mom would approve of her son getting involved with her again.

Raleigh took out his phone, but before he could press in Alma's number, he got another call. Her chest tightened when she saw the words *Unknown Caller* on the screen.

"Use your phone to record this," Raleigh in-sisted, and he waited until she had hit the re-cording function.

"Sheriff Lawton," a man said when Raleigh answered.

It wasn't a voice she recognized, and appar-ently neither did Raleigh because he snapped, "Who is this?"

"I'm the man who's going to make your day. You know that missing kid? The one that Han-nah Neal was carrying for that couple who hired her to be a surrogate," he added. "Well,

I got the kid. And before you ask, she's just fine."

Thea certainly hadn't expected that. Nor was she sure it was true.

"You've got the baby that's been missing?" Raleigh challenged. "You're sure about that, or is this some kind of hoax to extort some ransom money?"

"No hoax, and yeah, I'm sure."

"If that's true, where has the baby been all this time? She's been missing for a year."

"She's been in good hands with a nanny," the man said.

Thea prayed that was true. But that didn't mean the baby would remain in good hands, because this thug probably had demands. Money for sure. But maybe something more— like exchanging the baby for her. That's what Marco had wanted anyway, and this could be Buck, Marco's partner on the other end of the line.

If Buck or this snake did indeed want her, then Thea would try to make that happen. This had nothing to do with her being a cop. There was just no way she could allow the baby to be in the hands of a killer.

"You probably got questions," the man went on, "but you must know that I'm not gonna be real keen on answering them, especially since you're probably taping this and all. But here's the deal. You get the kid, no strings attached."

"Really? No strings?" Raleigh challenged.

"Not a one. If you want the kid, she's right outside the back door of the diner, the one that leads into the alley. My advice? Get there fast before I change my mind."

And with that, the caller hung up.

"You're not going out there," Raleigh said to Thea before she could even volunteer. "Stay put, and that's not up for negotiation."

Thea understood his concern. They'd nearly been killed just hours earlier, but she hadn't been the only one in the middle of that attack. Raleigh had been, too. Still, she didn't say anything because she knew it wasn't an argument she could win.

Raleigh drew his gun and hurried into the squad room. "Call the diner," he told Alice. "I don't want any of the employees or customers going outside the building, but there could be a baby at their back door."

Alice was in the process of making that call when Thea saw the front entrance of the diner open, and a woman in a waitress uniform started walking toward the sheriff's office.

She was holding an infant car seat, and there was indeed a baby strapped inside it.

Raleigh ran to the door, threw it open, and the moment the waitress reached him, he pulled her inside. "I heard a baby crying," she said, "and when I went to check it out, I found her. There's an envelope taped to the side of the seat, but I didn't touch it. I didn't unhook the straps, either."

That was smart of her, but Thea doubted there'd be any evidence to recover from it. Still, they had something that might link them back to who'd done this.

"Did you see anyone else back there or in the alley?" Raleigh asked the woman.

She shook her head. "Just the baby. Why would someone leave a precious little girl out there like that?"

"I don't know, but I'll find out," Raleigh assured her.

Thea went into the squad room so she could have a better look. The baby was wearing a pink dress and had blond curls. She was fussing and kicking her feet, but she seemed to be unharmed. Thank God.

"I need gloves," Raleigh told Alice, and the deputy ran to the supply cabinet to get him a pair.

Once Raleigh had them on, he took the car seat from the waitress, moving it to one of the desk tops. He clicked a picture of the carrier and baby before he removed the envelope. There was no letter or note inside, just two photos. And the sight of them caused Thea's breath to stall in her throat.

Because the first was a picture of Hannah. Alive. And she was holding a newborn baby. Judging from the looks of it, it was the baby she'd just delivered.

Raleigh moved on to the second photo, and even though Thea had tried to steel herself up for whatever it would be, the steeling didn't work. The sickening feeling of dread washed over her.

In this picture, Hannah was dead. Her lifeless body was sprawled out. And next to her was a man in a ski mask, holding the precious baby in his arms.

Chapter Ten

The nightmare woke Raleigh, and he jack-knifed in the bed. The images of an attack had been so real that his body had kicked up a huge amount of adrenaline, preparing itself for a fight. But there was no threat. He was alone in his bed, and his house was quiet.

Quiet but with the smell of coffee in the air.

He threw back the covers and checked the time. It was barely 6:00 a.m., which meant he'd gotten about five hours of sleep. Apparently though, Thea had gotten even less than that, since she was almost certainly the reason for the coffee scent. That meant she was probably up, working, something he should be doing.

Raleigh grabbed a quick shower, threw on some clothes and hurried into the kitchen. Thea was there all right, and there was a half-filled pot of coffee on the kitchen counter. But she was sacked out, her head on the table next to her open laptop and her phone.

The sound of his footsteps must have alerted her though because her eyes flew open, and she reached for her gun. Which wasn't there. Because she was wearing his pj's. Or rather pj's that belonged to him. Her brother hadn't packed her a pair of her own, so she'd had to use a pair of his.

For all of his adult life, Raleigh had only slept in boxers or gone commando, but for some reason his mother always gave him pajamas, slippers and robes as gifts. He'd never used any of them, but they looked darn good on Thea.

"Sorry," she mumbled. She stood and stretched, causing the blue plaid fabric to tighten across her breasts. Plus, she'd missed the two bottom buttons on the top, so he got a nice peep show of her stomach.

Yeah, the pj's looked good on her.

Raleigh felt his body clench, and to stop himself from ogling her, he got his mind on something else. "You couldn't sleep?" he asked, pouring himself a cup of coffee.

"I managed to get in a couple of hours, but I wanted to check on the baby. Well, both babies, actually. Rachel's an early riser because her pregnancy is getting to the uncomfortable stage, so she emailed me some updates. Sonya's baby is fine. And the baby that the waitress found yesterday is with social services and has had her DNA tested."

That was a start, but in addition to keeping both girls safe, they needed to know the identities of their parents. If the older baby was indeed the one that Hannah had carried, then the child would be given to the birth parents, the couple who'd hired Hannah to be their surrogate. It could be wonderful news for them.

Of course, that didn't change the fact that Hannah was dead.

Since Thea had already started her work day, Raleigh did, too. He took his laptop to the table and loaded his email, and he immediately saw one from the lab. According to the test they'd run, there were no prints on the car seat other than those of the waitress. And none on the envelope or the photos. Along with that, there were no fibers or trace evidence. Not good, but the photos would still be analyzed though to see if there was any visual evidence in the background.

Something that Raleigh had already been looking at.

Too bad he'd found nothing. However, he'd had the photos scanned, and he downloaded them from the storage files.

"Griff has been in touch with the San Antonio Fire Department," Thea continued. She got up to pour herself more coffee. "Both fires at the security company and fertility clinic were set with accelerants. Something we'd already suspected."

They had. Ditto for suspecting that Yvette would claim the money in the nightstand drawer was for emergencies, that there was no way she'd ever used the cash to pay a kidnapper. Yvette had also claimed that once there had been three grand in the envelope, but they'd tapped into it for various things.

As for the phone, Yvette insisted she had no idea why it was there. Since they still hadn't been able to get in touch with Nick, Raleigh didn't have anyone to confirm or deny what she'd said. And the phone wasn't going to be of much help because if it had been used to make or receive calls, all of that had been erased, and it had been wiped of any prints.

"I don't suppose you have any news about Buck?" Thea asked, sitting back down beside him again. "*Good news*—like the cops found and arrested him."

She looked at his laptop screen and groaned softly. That's because he had the photo of Hannah dead on the screen. Thea had seen it before, of course, but it never got easier to look at something like that.

"The killer was sick to take her picture," she mumbled and looked away.

Yeah, he was sick, but the ski-mask-wearing thug might have done that in case he ever had to prove that the baby was the one Hannah had delivered. A photo would have come in handy if there'd been a ransom demand. But there hadn't been.

Well, not until two days ago.

Raleigh pulled up the third picture, the one that'd been sent to Nick on his phone, and he positioned it side by side with the photo taken of Hannah when she was still alive. And holding the newborn that she'd almost certainly just delivered.

"They look like the same baby," Thea muttered.

Raleigh agreed, though the lab should be able to determine that. DNA, too. But that wouldn't answer his question of why the kidnapper/killer waited a year to return the little girl.

"At least the baby is healthy," Thea added. "The hospital said she's been well taken care of."

That was something at least, but it wouldn't

erase the hell the biological parents had gone through worrying about their missing child.

"Dalton's coordinating all the security cameras for that block around the diner," Raleigh said after glancing at his next email update.

No one had seen anyone leave the baby, but it was possible one of the cameras had picked up something. But even if they had footage of the person, Raleigh figured the guy was long gone. Something had caused him to give up the child—without collecting a penny—and that meant he was likely going on the run.

But why?

Maybe the guy felt that he was close to being caught. Or if it was Buck, he could have known about the APB and that he would be arrested for murder if he stayed around.

"We need to find the nanny who took care of the baby," Thea said. "If she's alive, that is."

Thea's voice cracked a little on those last

words, and she got up again, turning away from him. Since she wasn't looking at anything in particular, Raleigh figured she was dodging his gaze. That's why he stood, too. He took hold of her hand and eased her back around to face him.

There were tears in her eyes.

"Sometimes, it just gets to be too much," she whispered.

He felt the same way. The murders, the kidnappings, the fires and the attacks. And they still didn't know why this was happening. The problem was that it could get a whole lot worse.

Knowing it was a mistake, Raleigh pulled her into his arms and brushed a kiss on the top of her head. He kept it chaste. Well, as much as something like that could be between Thea and him. Which wasn't very chaste at all. He felt the immediate punch from the heat.

And tried to rein it in.

After all, they weren't in his office, where someone could come walking in at any minute. They were in his house, behind closed doors and alone. Plus, there were the memories of when they'd had sex just a few yards away on the sofa in the living room.

Thea looked up at him and frowned. "Should we try to talk ourselves out of this?" The corners of her mouth lifted, and it seemed as if she was going to use that half joke to move away from him.

She didn't.

That's because she kept staring at his mouth, and her body seemed to be issuing this silent invitation for him to kiss her. So that's what he did. Raleigh snapped her to him, and he pushed common sense right out the window when he pressed his mouth to hers.

There it was. More than just a mere kick

of attraction. As it always was with Thea, it started out scalding and just got hotter from there. That would have been good if this had been leading to sex. But it couldn't.

Raleigh repeated that.

Though he probably could have repeated it a hundred times and it wouldn't have helped. That's because Thea slipped her arms around his neck and pulled him down even lower so he could deepen the kiss.

The need came, sliding right through him and making him want to take this up a notch. So he did. Without breaking the kiss, Raleigh turned her, backing her against the wall, and he made that need even more urgent when he slid his hand beneath her top.

No bra.

Hell, he was in trouble.

And he kept creating the trouble when he cupped her right breast and flicked his thumb over her nipple. It wasn't hard to find because it was already puckered and tight from arousal. He made that worse, too, by lowering his head and taking it into his mouth.

Thea made a moaning sound. It was all pleasure. She definitely didn't move away from him. In fact, she ran her hands down his back, pulling him closer and closer.

Raleigh lingered there awhile, tasting her, and he took the kisses lower. To her stomach. The waist of the pj's bottoms was loose on her, making it very easy for him to push down the fabric and keep kissing until he reached the top of her panties. A sane man would have stopped there, but he just pushed them down and kept kissing.

Thea cursed, the profanity probably aimed at him. Maybe at herself. But those sounds of pleasure kept urging him on. So did the sight of her when he got her panties low enough.

He'd made love to her this way before, but it'd been a long time.

Too long.

And maybe if he kept it to just this, he could convince himself that he hadn't crossed every line that shouldn't be crossed between them. But before Raleigh could take things to the next step, he heard a different sound. One he didn't want to hear. Because his phone was ringing.

Hell. Talk about losing focus.

Thea scrambled away from him and started fixing her clothes. Raleigh did some scrambling, too, and he whipped out his phone to see Dalton's name on the screen. Since it was too early for routine business, he knew this had to be important for his deputy to call him at home.

"What happened?" Raleigh asked when he

hit the answer button. And he hoped someone else wasn't dead or had been kidnapped.

"Nick O'Hara just walked in."

Well, at least the man was alive. Since no one had heard from him in twenty-four hours, Raleigh had started to think he was either dead or had fled because he was guilty of something.

"Mr. O'Hara's asking to talk to you," Dalton added a moment later. "I think you should come in because he says he needs to make a confession."

EVEN THOUGH IT was only a short drive from Raleigh's house to the sheriff's office, Thea was on edge for every second of the trip. But at least they might have answers soon. Well, they would if Nick's confession led them to a killer—either himself or someone he'd hired.

"We never did find a connection between Nick and Hannah," Thea reminded Raleigh.

Even though Raleigh's attention seemed to be on keeping watch around them, he made an immediate sound of agreement. "Maybe there isn't one. Sonya's murder could be a copycat killing. One that doesn't have anything to do with Hannah. Or Warren."

She wished that would turn out to be true. It wouldn't bring back either woman, but it might ease the guilt Warren was no doubt feeling since he believed he was the reason for both women dying.

"About what happened right before I got Dalton's call..." Raleigh tossed out there.

Thea certainly hadn't forgotten about it. They were within a heartbeat of having some form of sex. And Raleigh was almost certainly regretting it.

She was about to give him an out. To tell

him that being under the same roof had just stirred some old memories. But Raleigh continued before she could say anything.

"If we're together, alone, it'll happen again." He mumbled some profanity to go along with that.

Thea couldn't deny that, and she took a moment to try to figure out how to answer that. "I should stay at my own place tonight. Griff can arrange a protection detail—"

"No," Raleigh interrupted. He looked at her. It was barely a glance, but he managed to put a lot of emotions into such a brief look. She saw the frustration. Even some anger. But she also saw the heat. "I want you in my bed, and your being somewhere else isn't going to change that."

Well, the man certainly knew how to take her breath away. And complicate things. Especially since it was obvious that neither of them should be thinking about sex right now. It was also obvious that it was going to happen whether or not it made a mess out of this situation.

Thankfully, Thea didn't have to say anything else because Raleigh pulled to a stop in front of the sheriff's office. Later though, there'd need to be a discussion about this. Or perhaps this attraction was past the discussion point.

Maybe she should just go for it. A hot, sweaty round of ex-sex with Raleigh might burn up some of this energy and cool down some of this fire between them. But then she looked at him and decided it was best if she didn't lie to herself. Sex wouldn't cool down anything. It would only remind her of what she'd once had with Raleigh.

And she wanted that again.

"Yeah," he said as if he knew exactly what she was thinking.

He didn't add more. Instead, Raleigh hurried her out of the cruiser and into the squad room, where she immediately spotted Nick. Not alone, either.

Simon was standing next to him.

"My client wants to talk to you," Simon greeted.

"Your client?" Raleigh challenged.

Nick nodded and rubbed his hand over his face. He definitely didn't look like the polished businessman who'd first shown up in Durango Ridge. No. Judging from his rumpled hair and clothes, he'd had a rough time. Thea knew exactly how he felt. But what she didn't understand was why he'd hired Simon.

Simon definitely seemed to be all right with the arrangement though.

The man was practically gloating, maybe

because he believed this was some kind of dig against Raleigh and her. However, Thea was far less interested in Nick's choice of attorney than she was in why he felt he needed a lawyer in the first place. Maybe he did intend on confessing to murder.

"This way," Raleigh said, leading Simon and Nick toward an interview room. He motioned for Thea to come, as well.

She braced herself for Simon or even Nick to object to her being there. After all, this wasn't her jurisdiction. But neither man brought it up when she followed them into the room.

Simon and Nick sat at the table, and Raleigh took the seat across from them. "What's this all about?" Raleigh asked.

Despite the fact that Nick had been the one to ask for this meeting, he didn't jump right into an explanation. He groaned. "I was having an affair with Sonya," he finally blurted out.

Along with the shock of hearing that, Thea got a heavy feeling in her stomach. Sonya had never hinted of an affair. Of course, that didn't mean it hadn't happened.

"I'm going to want to hear a lot more about this," Raleigh insisted.

Nick didn't continue though until Simon whispered something in his ear. "The affair started shortly after we met. Right after Sonya got confirmation that she was pregnant."

Raleigh glanced at her, probably to see if she'd had any inkling, but Thea had to shake her head.

"I fell in love with Sonya," Nick went on. "And that's the reason I wasn't too enthusiastic when I thought I'd be raising my and Yvette's child. My marriage was in trouble— and don't blame Sonya for that. I had fallen out of love with my wife before I even met Sonya."

Thea couldn't believe what she was hearing. "Then why the heck did you agree to a surrogate pregnancy?"

Again, Simon whispered something to Nick, and it was Simon who continued. "Mr. O'Hara has come here in good faith, to set the record straight. I won't tolerate either of you judging him for his extramarital involvement."

Raleigh gave both of them a blank stare. "No judging. I'll leave that to a jury."

"A jury?" Nick snapped, jumping to his feet, but Simon pulled him right back in the chair.

"Are you saying you're going to arrest my client?" Simon asked, his tone smug because he knew an affair alone wouldn't be enough of a motive to charge Nick with Sonya's murder.

But maybe there was something else here.

"No arrest. Not yet," Raleigh added. "Right

now though, I see a big red flag for *your client.* He's just admitted to an affair with a woman who was murdered. An affair he waited two days to tell us about. And now he admits to a rocky marriage. Is he here to confess to murder or to point the finger at his wife?"

"I didn't kill Sonya," Nick insisted, and he left it at that. Which meant he likely was going to try to pin this on Yvette.

And she might have done it, too.

"Yvette knew about the affair?" Thea asked.

Nick took his time answering. "I never told her, but I believe she found out and killed Sonya."

Raleigh didn't take that at face value. With his raised eyebrows, he looked skeptical. "You got any proof that Yvette did it?"

"She argued with Sonya the morning of the murder," Nick was quick to remind them.

"Yes, because Yvette found out the baby

wasn't hers and that Sonya was thinking about keeping the child," Raleigh reminded him right back. "In that case, I think it was justified for Yvette to be upset." He leaned forward, his cop's stare on Nick. "So, how did you react when you found out the baby was yours and Sonya's?"

Nick exchanged glances with Simon before he said anything. "I was, well, shocked."

It was an interesting reaction, considering Nick had just talked about being in love with Sonya. There was something else going on here, and Raleigh picked up on it, too.

"I'm going out on a limb here, but I don't think you had plans to ever divorce Yvette," Raleigh started. "Maybe because she comes from money? I remember her saying you two ran her late father's successful real estate company. So, did you sign a prenup?"

Bingo. Nick didn't have to verbally confirm

that for Thea to know it was true, and that led her to a problem that Sonya's pregnancy could have created.

"If Yvette found out Sonya was carrying your baby, she might have thought the child was the result of your affair," Thea suggested. "That would have given her grounds for a divorce. Of course, the affair alone would have also done that, but the baby would be proof that she could use in a court battle. And if she divorced you, you'd be broke and without a job."

That lit an angry fire in Nick's eyes. It didn't have Simon remaining calm, either. "Are you accusing me of setting up Yvette to take the blame for Sonya's murder?" Nick snarled.

"If Deputy Morris isn't accusing you, then I am," Raleigh fired back. "You've got a big motive for wanting Yvette behind bars. Plus, you lied to us. And let's get into the part about you knowing that Sonya's baby was yours, and yet you claimed it wasn't, that Thea and I had gotten the wrong child from Marco."

Nick huffed. "That was an honest mistake. The baby didn't look like Sonya and me, and I thought the other baby did. I didn't know it was a hoax to milk money from me."

Any money would have come from Yvette. If she had fallen for the hoax, that is. She hadn't. Yvette had continued to try to stake her claim to the baby Raleigh and she had rescued. And she'd done that despite the fact that the baby wasn't biologically hers. Maybe because she was desperate to be a mother, but Thea wondered if there was another reason.

Yvette could have somehow planned to use the child to get back at her cheating husband.

"My client has voluntarily explained everything to you," Simon concluded, and he stood. "I'm assuming he's free to go."

"No, he's not." Raleigh motioned for Nick to

sit back down. "Tell me about the money that SAPD found in your nightstand drawer. And the phone between the mattresses."

Nick had already opened his mouth to answer until Raleigh added the last part. His mouth tightened, telling them that the man hadn't *explained everything* after all. "The money is for emergencies," Nick said after a long pause. "The phone was the one I used to call Sonya. I couldn't use my regular cell because Yvette would have seen Sonya's number on the bill."

"Now, are you satisfied?" Simon snapped at Raleigh.

"No. I'm more than a little concerned that you're the attorney for two suspects in this murder investigation."

"A suspect?" Nick howled.

Raleigh looked him straight in the eyes. "You heard me. If you're innocent, I'll apologize, but there'll be an asterisk by it because you withheld information about your affair with the victim." Raleigh stood. "Now you're free to go."

Thea and Raleigh walked out, leaving Nick still grumbling about being a suspect. Too bad they didn't have anything to hold the man, but other than circumstantial evidence, there was nothing to tie him to the crime of either Sonya's murder or the kidnapping.

"I'll call the lab and ask them to take another look at that cell phone the cops found between the mattresses," Raleigh said as they went back toward his office. "The calls were all erased, but maybe there's a storage cache they can find. I also need to have another chat with Yvette about the prenup and to find out if she knew anything about the affair."

Yes, because the affair could give Yvette motive for murdering Sonya.

Raleigh reached for his phone, but he stopped when they got to his office. That's because it wasn't empty.

His mother was there.

Thea checked the time to make sure it wasn't later than she thought. It wasn't. It wasn't even seven thirty yet. Pretty early for a visit, which meant something could be wrong.

"Dalton said Simon was here." Alma's voice was a little shaky. Actually, the same applied to her, too. She had a wadded up tissue in her hand, and Thea thought she might have been crying.

Raleigh nodded. "He's with a new client."

"I'll wait out here while you two talk," Thea offered.

But Alma immediately shook her head. "No. Please come in. Both of you. But shut the door. I don't want Simon to know I'm here."

Well, this was interesting, considering that

Simon was not only Alma's longtime friend but her lawyer.

"Did something happen?" Raleigh asked once Thea and he were inside the office. He also shut the door.

His mother volleyed some nervous glances at him. "It's about Warren," Alma said after a very long hesitation.

Thea wanted to groan, and she hoped Alma wasn't about to try to accuse Warren of some crime.

"I wrote a letter to Warren," Alma went on when Raleigh and Thea just stared at her. "It was something I didn't want him to read until after my death."

Raleigh's forehead bunched up, and Thea's was certain that hers did, too. "What kind of letter?" Raleigh pressed. He wasn't using the same rough tone he did with Nick, but he was clearly concerned about this.

Alma was concerned, too, because she needed to use that tissue to dab at her eyes. "You're not going to like it, but I told Warren that I loved him. And I still do."

Raleigh mumbled some profanity. "He hurt you."

Alma nodded, blinked back tears. "And I'm sure I hurt his wife. Remember, I knew he was married, and I still kept seeing him."

Thea had to wonder if Sonya had felt the same way about Nick. She hoped it was love anyway and that the love hadn't soured to the point that it would make Nick want to kill her.

When Alma's tears continued, Raleigh went to her and pulled her into his arms. He brushed a kiss on the top of her head. "Why are you telling me this? Did something happen with the letter?"

"Yes, I believe something did."

Thea prayed that Warren's wife hadn't seen it. She was just now back on her feet, recovering from a mental breakdown, and it wouldn't help for her to see something like that.

Alma eased back from Raleigh to face both of them. "I was going to put the letter in the safe in my office, but I got busy doing something else and left it on my desk when I went out to meet with one of the new hands. While I was gone, Ruby said that Simon arrived, and he went into my office."

"Ruby?" Thea asked.

"My housekeeper. She said, when she looked in my office, that Simon was reading the letter, and that he got very mad and stormed out. Ruby was going to tell me, but then her daughter got sick, and she had to leave. It must have slipped her mind because she didn't tell me about it until this morning."

So Simon had seen, in writing, that Alma still had feelings for Warren. That definitely wouldn't have sit well with him. But maybe it had done something much, much more.

"When did all this happen?" Raleigh asked. "When did Simon read the letter?"

Alma's mouth began to tremble. "The same morning that Sonya was murdered."

Oh, mercy. Maybe that was a coincidence, but it was too strong of a connection to dismiss it.

"I suppose you'll have to ask Simon about it?" Alma said to her son.

"Yes." Obviously giving that some thought, Raleigh stayed quiet a moment. "But not now. Not while you're here." He hugged her. "Just go on home, and I'll take care of it."

But Alma didn't budge. "Are you disappointed with me?" she asked him.

"No. I'm not disappointed," Raleigh assured her. And Thea believed that was the truth.

"Do you think I'm a fool for still having these feelings for Warren?" Alma aimed that second question at Thea.

Thea sighed and repeated Raleigh's "no."

Alma wasn't a fool. She was just a woman who couldn't get over her feelings for a man— something Thea could certainly relate to.

Raleigh opened the door and looked out, no doubt checking to make sure Simon wasn't out there. He wasn't, so Raleigh opened the door even wider. "You want me to have one of the deputies drive you home?" he asked her.

His mother shook her head and gave his hand a gentle squeeze. "I'll be fine. I just need some time to myself."

Thea watched the woman walk out, and she felt a strange mix of feelings. Resentment at the part Alma had played in nearly destroying Warren's marriage. But Thea felt empathy, too. She looked at Raleigh to tell him that, but Dalton came toward them.

"The lab just sent over the DNA results on the newborn," Dalton said. He handed Raleigh the report. "And as you can see, it's not what we were expecting."

Chapter Eleven

Raleigh read through the lab report, shook his head and read it again. What the heck was going on?

"The baby isn't Nick's," Thea said as she looked at the DNA results. "She's Sonya and Dr. Sheridan's."

Dalton had been right about them not expecting this. "How did the lab even have Dr. Sheridan's DNA to do the comparison?" Raleigh asked Dalton. And that was just the first of many questions he had.

"He was in the system because he worked in a federal prison for a short time, so when the baby's DNA didn't match Nick's, the lab tech just fed the results through the database. Dr. Sheridan fathered that baby."

It didn't take Raleigh long to figure out how this could have happened. Madison had already told them that Yvette's harvested eggs had been misplaced. Well, maybe Nick's semen had been, too. Dr. Sheridan could have substituted his own to make up for the mistake.

Or he'd been asked to do that by someone.

The only person in this equation who wasn't so eager for that baby to be conceived was Nick. That could mean he was in on this, and if so, he'd have a strong motive to kill the doctor if Sheridan had decided to come clean with Yvette.

"In case Nick's the one behind this, we need to dig into Dr. Sheridan's bank account and see if he was paid off for his part in the botched in vitro," Raleigh told Dalton. "We know there were no large sums of money taken from the O'Haras' bank account, but see if you can figure out another way for Nick to have gotten his hands on some cash about nine months ago."

"I'll get right on that," Dalton said as he went back to his desk.

"You really think Nick killed Sonya?" Thea asked.

"Maybe. If she'd tried to break things off with him, he could have been enraged enough to do something like that. There weren't any recordings of her and Nick's conversations, so we really don't know how things were between them."

She made a sound of agreement. "And then Nick could have killed Dr. Sheridan and burned down the clinic and the security company to cover his tracks." She paused. "Of course, Yvette could have hired someone to do the murders to set up her husband. If she was upset enough about the affair, she might have wanted to get revenge."

True. But it was also possible that the botched in vitro had nothing to do with the murders or the attacks. If so, then this all went back to Simon. And unlike Nick and Yvette, Simon did have a connection to one of the hired guns.

Raleigh's phone rang, and considering everything that was going on, he halfway expected to see *Unknown Caller* on the screen. But it was a familiar name.

Warren.

Raleigh wasn't especially eager to talk to him, but since this could be about the investigation, he answered it right away.

"I was driving into Durango Ridge to check on Thea," Warren immediately said, "and I saw your mom's car parked on the side of the road."

Raleigh's heart went into overdrive, especially when he heard his mother yelling in the background. "Is she all right?" He couldn't ask that fast enough.

"She's not hurt or anything like that, but she's crying and clearly upset. She tried to drive off, but I took away her keys. I didn't think she should be behind the wheel like that." Warren paused. "And now she's pulled a gun on me."

Raleigh didn't even bother to hold back the profanity. "I'm on the way. Where are you exactly?"

"About a quarter of a mile south of the turn for Alma's ranch."

Raleigh knew the spot. "Tell her not to do anything stupid, that I'll be right there."

He put away his phone and took out the keys

for the cruiser parked right out front, but that's when he realized Thea was following him.

"You're not going out there alone," she insisted.

Hell. Now he had to worry about both his mother and Thea. And Warren. He didn't like the man, but he darn sure didn't want his mother to end up in jail for shooting him. Later, he'd kick himself for not having one of the deputies escort Alma home, but for now, he needed to get to her and hopefully defuse a bad situation.

"Come with us," Raleigh told Dalton. He hated to pull Dalton away from the pile of work that was on his desk, but after what happened at the security company, Raleigh didn't want to take any chances.

After Raleigh told Alice what was going on, Dalton, Thea and he hurried outside to the cruiser. Raleigh got behind the wheel, and with Dalton at shotgun, Thea got in the back. Raleigh turned on the flashing lights and siren so he could get down Main Street as fast as possible.

"What do you think happened to your mom?" Thea asked.

He doubted it was anything other than what Alma had already told them. That she was worried about Simon having read the letter. That had already brought his mother to tears before she'd come to the sheriff's office, and those tears had obviously continued after she left.

"I think my mom is worried that Simon murdered Sonya, maybe Hannah, too, and now she's blaming herself." Of course, that didn't explain why she'd pull a gun on a man she still loved, but it could be she'd gotten so hysterical that she didn't know what she was doing. Which made this situation even more dangerous.

Even though it was only a couple of miles, it seemed to take forever for them to get there, and by the time they arrived, Raleigh could feel his pulse drumming in his ears. What he saw sure didn't help with that, either.

Alma's car was indeed there. His mom had pulled off into a narrow clearing that was in front of a cattle gate and pasture. At least she hadn't stopped on the road. Warren's truck was parked just behind Alma's car, and Dalton pulled to a stop behind it since the road shoulder was too narrow to park ahead of the vehicles.

Warren was there, too. He was standing by the driver's-side door of Alma's car. He had his hands raised in the air. Alma was inside, still behind the wheel, and she did indeed have a gun aimed at Warren. The gun was a

Smith & Wesson that he knew his mom kept in her glove compartment.

Raleigh's first instinct was to bolt from the cruiser, but he glanced around first. Something he'd been doing during the whole drive. But he didn't see anyone. Maybe it would stay that way, though this was the road that led into town, so someone would no doubt eventually drive by.

He glanced back at Thea to tell her to stay put, but she was already getting out. And he couldn't blame her. She loved Warren and was probably afraid for his life.

Raleigh and Dalton got out as well, and Raleigh maneuvered himself in front of Thea. He didn't draw his gun, but Dalton did.

"I didn't want Warren to call you," his mom immediately said.

"Then you shouldn't have pulled a gun on him. Put it away, *now*," Raleigh ordered, and he was sure he sounded more like a sheriff than her son. "What the heck is going on here?"

Alma was crying all right, the tears streaming down her face, and she shook her head. "I just want my keys so I can go home, and he wouldn't give them to me."

But Warren handed them to Raleigh just as Thea went to Warren's side.

"You're not driving home like this," Raleigh told his mother. "And Warren was right to do what he did." And no, hell didn't freeze over because he'd taken his *father's* side on this.

"Alma's not thinking straight. She wouldn't have shot me though," Warren insisted.

Probably not, but it was too big of a risk to take. That's why Raleigh held out his hand for his mother to give him the gun. She didn't jump to do that, but he didn't want to try to wrench it from her hand and end up risking her pulling the trigger by accident. She finally gave it to him and then collapsed with a hoarse sob against the steering wheel.

"This is all my fault," Alma managed to say, though it had to be hard to talk with her having to drag in her breath like that. "Simon did this for me."

Warren didn't seem surprised by that comment, which meant it'd likely been the topic of their conversation before things had taken a very bad turn.

"Simon might not have done anything wrong," Raleigh explained. "Especially nothing that had anything to do with you. We have two other solid suspects in Sonya's murder."

His mother lifted her head, blinked and stared at him. "Are you just saying that to make me feel better?"

"No. I'm saying it because it's true. And

even if it wasn't, you aren't responsible for what Simon does or doesn't do."

She shook her head again. "But the letter…"

Now, Warren did show some surprise. He frowned when he looked at Raleigh. "What letter?"

Since it wasn't his place to answer that, Raleigh just waited for his mom to say something, but she waved it off. "It doesn't matter. I shouldn't have written the letter in the first place."

Alma wiped away her tears and sat up straight. She was probably trying to look strong enough to drive, but Raleigh wasn't buying it.

"Are you going to press charges for her pulling the gun on you?" Raleigh asked Warren.

"No." He fixed his gaze on Alma. "I did wrong by her. By you," he added to Raleigh. "I deserve anything the two of you dish out."

Well, he didn't deserve to be shot, and Raleigh considered it progress that he felt that way. He mumbled a thanks for Warren not pressing those charges, and then he had a quick debate about how to handle this. He couldn't allow his mother to go home alone, and he didn't think handing her off to Dalton was a good idea.

"I need to drive my mother home," Raleigh finally said to Thea. "You can go back to town with Dalton. Or Warren."

Thea seemed to have a debate with herself, too. She volleyed glances at all of them. "Why don't Dalton and I go with you to take Alma home? We could use the cruiser."

Raleigh didn't have to guess why she would suggest that. It was bullet resistant, and they could be attacked along the way. It was a good idea, but what wasn't good was extending the invitation for Warren to go with them. Warren must have sensed what Raleigh was thinking because he tipped his head to his truck.

"I'll be going," Warren said. "Now that I know Thea's okay, I need to be getting home." He hugged her and headed to his truck.

"I made a fool of myself," Alma mumbled, and the tears started again when Warren drove away.

Despite the crying, Raleigh didn't want to wait around to calm her down again, so he opened her door. "Come on. I'll have someone from the ranch come back and get your car."

His mom didn't argue with him about that, thank God, and he got her moving to the cruiser. However, he didn't get far. Only a few steps. Before Raleigh heard something that he didn't want to hear.

A gunshot.

At first Thea thought the sound was a car backfiring, but she glanced up the road and saw that Warren's truck was already out of sight. And there wasn't another vehicle with a running engine anywhere around.

Raleigh obviously knew what it was though because, in the split second that followed the shot, he hooked his arms around her and his mother, and he pulled them to the ground.

Alma made a sharp gasp of pain, and Thea immediately had a terrifying thought—that the woman had been shot. But Alma had hit her head during the fall. She'd have a scrape on her cheek, but it was far better than the alternative.

Another shot came, and this one slammed into the ground, much too close to where they were.

Raleigh's gaze was firing all around. He was obviously trying to pinpoint the location of the shooter. Since Dalton was doing the same thing, Thea hooked her arm around Alma's waist and pulled the woman behind the back of her car. It wasn't ideal cover, but at least they weren't out in the open.

But Raleigh and Dalton were.

"Get down!" Thea shouted to them just as two more shots came right at them. The bullets tore into the asphalt and the gravel shoulder of the road.

Raleigh and Dalton stayed low and they scrambled toward the back of the vehicle with Alma and her. Thea had already drawn her gun, but she had no idea where to even return fire.

"You see the shooter?" she asked Raleigh.

"He's somewhere across the road. Call for backup."

Thea did that. She called the sheriff's office and got Alice. The deputy assured her that she'd come right out, but Thea reminded her to approach with caution. She didn't want anyone else killed.

Mercy. This confirmed to Thea she was the target.

Of course, Thea had known that when Marco had taken her at gunpoint, but this reminder hit her like a Mack truck slamming into her. This wasn't just about cops being in the line of fire. Raleigh's mom could be hurt, or worse.

"Raleigh!" Alma shouted. "Don't let those bullets hit you."

Easier said than done. Three more shots came, one right behind the other.

While she positioned her body over Alma's to keep the woman on the ground, Thea lifted her head enough to glance at the direction of the shots. And she groaned. Because there were way too many trees and even some large rocks. The shooter could be behind any one of them.

"I swear, I didn't see a gunman," Alma insisted. "Where did he come from?"

Thea figured he'd parked on a ranch trail just off the pasture and then used the rocks and trees for cover to get into position. Maybe he'd even been following Alma because it would have been easier to get to the older woman than it was Raleigh and her. With Alma's state of mind, she might not have even noticed if a stranger was behind her vehicle.

The next bullet slammed into Alma's car, shattering the window on the rear-passenger's side, and it sent glass flying at Dalton. He moved even farther back, but it wasn't enough. Dalton, and the rest of them, could still be hit.

Thea glanced behind them to try to figure out what to do. Now that Warren's truck was gone, there was an open space between the car and the cruiser. It was plenty big enough for them to be easy targets if they went running out there. But there might be another way around this.

"I can get to the cruiser and pull it up in front of you," Thea suggested.

Raleigh looked back at her, and even though he didn't give her a flat look, it was close. "You're not going there. And if you ignore my order and try it, I will go after you. That means, we'd both get shot."

Thea wanted to believe he was bluffing, but she doubted that he was. No way could she risk something like that. She couldn't lose Raleigh.

Even if he wasn't hers to lose.

"Stay down," Raleigh told her. "And make sure my mom stays put, too."

Thea was trying to do just that, but Alma kept calling out to Raleigh to be careful, and she was squirming so she could look at him, probably to make sure he was okay. Thea couldn't fault the woman for that. Raleigh was her only son, but she needed Alma to cooperate so she could help Raleigh return fire—if they got a chance to do that.

"Raleigh's a good cop," Thea reminded Alma. "Please stay down so I can help him."

Alma looked up at her, their gazes connecting, and even though it seemed to be the last thing the woman wanted to do, she nodded and quit struggling. She practically went limp on the ground.

Thea pivoted, still staying close to Alma but moving to the side so she stood a chance of having a clean shot. She tried again to pinpoint the shooter.

And she did.

Just as Raleigh and Dalton did, too—thanks to the sunlight glinting off the shooter's gun. He was in the center of the pasture, behind one of the big rocks. The rock was the perfect cover, but he had to lean out to shoot at them.

She waited, her heart pounding and her breath so thin that her chest was hurting. But Thea reminded herself that she'd been trained for this, and the stakes were too high for her to fail.

Dalton and Raleigh were obviously waiting, too, and both had their guns pointed in the direction of the shooter. The seconds crawled by, maybe because the guy was reloading, but Thea finally saw him. He moved out from behind the rock, already taking aim at them.

But Dalton, Raleigh and Thea all fired, their shots blending into a loud, thick blast that was deafening. They each fired several more times before she saw a man wearing a ski mask tumble out onto the ground.

They waited with the silence closing in around them. Raleigh was no doubt waiting to make sure the guy was actually dead and that he didn't have a partner waiting in the wings to gun them down when they moved.

She heard the sirens and glanced at the road to see the cruiser flying toward them. Alice, probably. Dalton verified that with a call to his fellow deputy, and Alice pulled to a stop directly in front of them.

Raleigh moved fast to get Alma into the cruiser. "Stay with her," he added to Thea. "I need to see if this guy is alive. If he is, we might finally know who's been trying to kill us."

Chapter Twelve

Raleigh stood at his kitchen counter and tossed back the shot of straight whiskey. It wasn't enough alcohol to cloud his head, but he hoped it would take off the edge. The adrenaline from the attack hadn't zapped nearly enough of this raw energy he was feeling.

Along with the frustration.

Because the shooter, Buck Tanner, was dead.

And that meant he hadn't been able to tell them who'd hired him. Not that he necessarily would have wanted to do that, but

Raleigh would have figured out a way to get him to talk.

But now that option was gone, and they were back to square one. Well, with the exception that the two men who'd killed Sonya and kidnapped the baby were dead. That would have felt like some kind of justice if they'd managed to catch the hired thugs' boss, too.

"Did it help?" he heard Thea ask. He glanced over his shoulder to see Thea walking into the living room.

She was in his pj's again.

Obviously, she'd just gotten out of the shower because she was using a towel to dry her wet hair, and she tipped her head to the glass he was still holding.

"The jury's out on that," he said. He lifted the bottle. "You want a shot?"

"No, thanks. I'll probably just grab some-

Delores Fossen 303

thing to eat and crash. Unless you think we'll need to go back into your office tonight."

He shook his head. With the exception of the DNA on the second baby, they weren't waiting on any lab results, and there were no reports from SAPD on the fires at the security company and fertility clinic.

But there was some bad news he needed to tell Thea.

Since there was no easy way to put this, Raleigh just turned to face her and blurted it out. "Dan Shaw's body turned up about a mile from the security company." The very one the man had owned. "He died from two gunshots to the head."

Thea's breath hitched, and her shoulders dropped. Even though she hadn't personally known him, that didn't matter. Dan Shaw was dead because someone, probably Buck Tanner, had taken him hostage so he could escape.

"I think I'll have that drink now," she said, her voice shaky. She didn't look too steady, either.

Raleigh grabbed another glass from the cabinet, poured her a shot, and when she reached for it, that's when he noticed the bandage on the palm of her hand. She quickly tried to hide it beneath the sleeve of the bulky pj's, but he caught on to her wrist and had a better look.

"It's nothing." She pulled back her hand. "I just cut it on a rock or something when I fell. I didn't even notice it until we were away from the scene."

Even though Raleigh knew it could have been much worse, it twisted his stomach to know she'd been hurt. He'd seen the blood on her clothes, of course. That's why she'd taken a shower and put her clothes in the washer as soon as they'd gotten to his house, but he'd thought the blood was his mom's—from the scrape she gotten when he'd pushed them to the ground.

"It's nothing," Thea repeated. She had a sip of the whiskey and grimaced, but that bad reaction didn't stop her from finishing off the rest of the shot.

Since looking at that bandage wasn't helping with that raw energy bubbling inside him, he opened the bag of takeout he'd gotten from the diner. Burgers and fries. It smelled good, but Raleigh doubted it would sit well with the knots in his stomach. Still, he wanted Thea to eat, so he put the food on some plates and set them on the table.

Thea glanced at the food and made another face. Not quite a grimace this time, but it was close. But she sat down and picked up one of the fries.

"Did you call your mom while I was in the shower?" she asked.

He nodded. "Like you, she's insisting she's okay. I doubt it's true in either your case or hers."

Thea lifted her shoulder. "My offer still stands. If you want to stay the night with her, I can go to my brother's."

She had indeed made that offer, but Sonya's baby was with Griff, Rachel and a Texas Ranger for extra protection. There'd been no attacks directed at the newborn, and Raleigh wanted to keep it that way. If Thea went there or to the McCall Ranch, the danger might go with her.

Of course, an attack could happen here, too, and that's why Raleigh had closed the gate that led to his house. He'd also alerted the hands who worked with his horses to report anything suspicious to him. Added to that, he'd turned on his security system.

Because the killer was still out there.

Raleigh didn't believe for a second that Marco and Buck had put this together themselves. No. Their boss was probably gathering another team of hired guns, and Raleigh had to be ready for whatever the snake threw at them.

"Alice is staying with my mom," he added. "And the ranch hands there will keep watch."

She nodded, took a tiny bite of the french fry and put it back on the plate. "What will happen to Sonya's baby?" she asked. "Both of her biological parents are dead, and Yvette and Nick don't have a claim on her, thank goodness."

Yeah, that definitely qualified as a *thank goodness*. Both the O'Haras were suspects, and he didn't want them getting anywhere near the baby.

"Social services is contacting Sonya's and Dr. Sheridan's next of kin. Sonya has an aunt who she was close to, and she's already asked about taking the baby."

Thea made a sound of approval but then frowned. Maybe because she'd gotten attached to the little girl when she'd been taking care of her. She tried the fry again, tossed it right back down and got up to go to the window. He'd closed all the blinds and curtains, but she lifted the edge of the blind and looked out.

"We can't live like this," she said. There'd been weariness in her voice earlier, but it had gone up a notch. "We have to know who's behind the attacks." She stayed quiet a moment and then turned back to him. "Why don't we set a trap, using me as bait."

Hell. Raleigh had figured this was coming, and Thea had to know he was going to nix it. He pushed back his plate and went to her. "I'm not going to watch you die so I can catch a killer."

"He or she wouldn't be able to kill me if we did this right. Just hear me out," she added when he opened his mouth to argue. "We could get the word out that I need to go see Warren, that it's some kind of emergency. The killer would probably set up another attack somewhere on the road. But we'd be ready. We could have some of the deputies hiding in the cruiser."

That wouldn't stop her from being killed. Heck, it could get the deputies killed, too.

"This could work," she went on, and he could tell that she wasn't just going to give up on this.

And that's why Raleigh kissed her.

It was playing dirty, but he couldn't listen to Thea talk about sacrificing herself to put an end to this. He kept the kiss short, and he eased back, fully expecting her to yell or even push him away.

She didn't.

Thea stared at him. A long time. And with their gazes locked, she caught on to the front of his shirt, wadding it up in her left hand as she dragged him back to her.

It was Thea who continued the kiss.

FROM THE MOMENT Thea had seen Raleigh in the kitchen, she'd known this kiss was going to happen. There was just too much energy sizzling between them. Too much emotion.

And too much frustration.

Raleigh seemed to try to cure all of that with the kiss. In one quick motion, she was in his arms, and the urgency of his mouth on hers let her know that neither of them were going to stop this. Even if they regretted it. Which they would.

Well, Raleigh would anyway.

Thea wasn't sure she could regret something

like this that felt so right. Of course, it'd always felt right when she was with Raleigh. It'd been that way for her even when she'd been with him after learning the truth about Warren's affair. Not telling Raleigh had caused her to lose him, and she'd thought she would never be with him like this again. But she was wrong. It was happening, and it was happening fast.

The kiss became hotter, more intense, and it didn't take minutes but rather mere seconds. Thea just let herself go with it when he pulled her deeper into his arms so that their bodies were touching. It was an incredible sensation with him touching her, but it soon wasn't enough. She needed more.

Thankfully, Raleigh didn't have trouble giving her that.

He popped open the buttons on the loose pajama top she was wearing, and he slipped his hand inside. She hadn't put on a bra after her shower, and without the barrier of any clothes, Raleigh lowered his head and moved the kisses to her breasts.

Yes, this was *more*.

Raleigh kept on giving, too, when he pushed down the bottom of the pj's. She was wearing panties, but he also slid them down her legs, leaving her practically naked. If she hadn't been so desperate for him, that might have bothered her, but Raleigh didn't give her a chance to remember who she was much less the fact that she was undressed, and he wasn't.

He kissed her. In many places. Touched her, too. And Thea let herself be swept up into the sensations that came wave after wave. Every inch of her wanted him more than her next breath, but despite the burning need, Raleigh just kept up with the maddening foreplay.

When she could take no more, Thea did

something about his clothes. It was hard to get his buttons undone while still kissing, but she managed it and got a very nice reward. Her hands on his bare chest.

He wasn't overly muscled, but he was toned and tight. Perfect. But then, she thought that "perfect" label applied to many things when it came to Raleigh. Thea kissed his neck and chest.

She would have kept going as he'd done, but he pulled her back up to him, and when their eyes met, Thea recognized the look he gave her. He was giving her an out if she wanted to stop.

She didn't.

So she went straight back to him. This time though, there was no more foreplay—something that her on-fire body was thankful for. Raleigh scooped her up and carried her straight to his room. The moment he had her on the bed, he took a condom from his nightstand drawer.

He moved onto the bed with her, the mattress giving way to their combined weight, and she helped him slide off his boots and jeans. His boxers, too. Everything was frantic now, their movements feverish from the need. He didn't waste a second after he put on the condom.

Raleigh pushed into her.

The pleasure raced through her, leaving her speechless. And breathless. But she could certainly feel, and the feelings soared when he started to move inside her.

The memories came. No way to stop them. They'd been together like this many times, but each of those times had always had the same intensity as the first. This was no different. Except Thea knew that it might be their last. Once Raleigh came to his senses, he might regret this enough that it would never happen again.

A heartbreaking thought.

But it was a thought that quickly went out the window when his thrusts inside her got faster. Harder. Until the need and tension climbed higher and higher.

When Thea couldn't hang on any longer, when she could take no more, she let herself surrender to the pleasure. The climax rippled through her, and the only thing she could do was hold on and let it consume her.

Moments later, as he whispered her name, Raleigh buried his face against her neck, and he finished what they'd started.

Chapter Thirteen

Raleigh closed his eyes and tried to sleep—something that usually happened easily after great sex. And this had indeed been *great*. But the sleep wouldn't come because his mind wasn't nearly as satisfied as the rest of him.

Sex was going to complicate things between Thea and him. Of course, the kissing had already done that, but this would send it through the roof. If the timing had been better, he might have just gone back in for another round of sex and put his worries on the back burner. But the timing only added to the complication.

He got up, but he tried to be as quiet as possible so that he wouldn't wake Thea. However, when he glanced at her, she was wide-awake and staring at the ceiling. Judging from the expression on her face, she was having more than just doubts and regrets.

"Was it that bad?" he joked, and because he was stupid, he brushed one of those complicating kisses on her mouth.

"No." She looked him straight in the eyes. "The frown is because it wasn't bad."

Unfortunately, he understood that. If the old chemistry between them had gone cold, it would have made leaving the bed easier. The kiss she gave him back in return certainly didn't help, either, but Raleigh forced himself to move away from her so he could get dressed.

"I should be keeping watch," he reminded her. "And checking for updates. You should try to get some sleep though."

But Raleigh knew that probably wasn't going to happen, and he was right. Thea immediately got up, and she headed to the guest room. A few minutes later, when she came out, she had dressed. Not in pj's, either, but her jeans and shirt.

"I'll make us a pot of coffee," she said, heading for the kitchen.

Raleigh considered asking Thea if she wanted to talk about what happened, but she was probably just as unsettled about this as he was. Plus, there wasn't time to launch into a conversation because his phone rang.

The call got Thea's attention, and she turned away from the coffee maker to hurry toward him. She was probably expecting it to be bad news, and when Raleigh saw the name on the screen, he considered that, as well. That's because it was Alice calling, and since she was staying with Alma, this could mean his mother was upset again. Maybe this time though, Alma hadn't pulled a gun on the deputy.

When Raleigh answered the call, the first thing he heard was the loud clanging noise. It definitely wasn't something he wanted to hear because he was pretty sure it was the security alarm.

"I think someone broke into the house," Alice immediately said.

The news hit him hard, but Raleigh reminded himself that it could be a glitch in the system. Or maybe his mom had accidentally set it off. Still, it was hard not to feel the fear and panic.

"I've gone into your mom's bedroom with her," Alice added, "and I've locked the door."

"I'm on the way there right now," Raleigh assured her. "Text or call me with what's happening." Though for now he wanted Alice to focus only on keeping his mother safe.

He ended the call and reached for his holster and keys. Thea obviously heard what Alice had said because she, too, grabbed her gun and her phone. Raleigh didn't especially want her coming with him since they'd already been attacked twice while on the road, but he didn't have time to make other arrangements.

He went to the window and looked out. Nothing out of the ordinary, and he hoped it stayed that way.

"Hurry," he told Thea, and the moment he had his own security system disengaged, he got them out the door and into the cruiser that he'd parked right by his porch.

He half expected someone to shoot at them, but thankfully no bullets came their way. So he sped off, while keeping watch to make sure they weren't ambushed. Thea was keeping watch, too, but he handed her his phone. He didn't have to tell her to answer it right away if Alice called back. Thea would. But Raleigh hoped that when Alice did contact them that it would be to say that it was a false alarm.

"Text my deputy Miguel," he instructed. "His number is in my contacts. He'll be at the office, and tell him I want him out at my mom's place."

It might be overkill, but that was better than being short of backup if this turned out to be an attack.

"How many ranch hands does Alma have on the grounds?" Thea asked after she'd fired off a text to Miguel.

"Two right now. She has a lot more who work for her, but they don't live there." Though he might end up calling a couple of them, too.

It was pitch-black, just a sliver of a moon, and there were no lights out on this rural road. No traffic, either, thank goodness, and that's why Raleigh went much faster than he would normally go.

His mom's ranch was only about five miles from his, so it didn't take long to get there. When he took the turn, the house came into view. All looked well, but Thea and he had to drive past some dark pastures. Since Buck Tanner had used a pasture to hide for his attack, that possibility was still fresh in Raleigh's mind.

His phone dinged with a text message. Then almost immediately dinged again. "Miguel's on the way," Thea relayed. "The second text is from Alice. She says no one has tried to break into the room, and she doesn't hear anyone in the house."

That was good, but it might be hard for his deputy to hear much of anything with the alarm still blaring. The only way to turn it off would be for her to go to the keypads at the front and back doors, and Raleigh preferred that she stay put.

Raleigh was about to tell Thea to let Alice know they were nearby, but he caught some movement from the corner of his eye. Thea must have seen it, too, because they both pivoted in that direction and took aim. Raleigh had braced himself for a ski-mask-wearing thug, but it wasn't.

It was Warren.

"Don't shoot," Warren said, leaning out from a tree that was right next to the road.

Raleigh lowered his window and glanced around to see if Warren was alone. He appeared to be.

"What are you doing here?" Thea asked, taking the question right out of Raleigh's mouth.

"I got a call from a criminal informant of mine. He said one of his buddies had been hired to kidnap Alma. That the person who hired the buddy wanted to do that to get back at me."

Raleigh huffed. "And you didn't call me with information like that?"

"I wasn't sure it was accurate. The guy isn't always reliable if he needs money for a fix. He needed money," Warren added.

And despite the tip not being reliable, Warren had come anyway. Later, Raleigh would press him as to why he'd done that and where he'd parked his truck, since it was nowhere in sight, but for now he needed to get to the house.

"My mom's with one of my deputies, but someone broke in. Thea and I are headed there now."

That put some alarm on Warren's face. "I didn't see anyone come onto the grounds, and I was keeping watch."

Later, Raleigh would want to know about

that, too. Because if there was indeed an intruder, it was possible he'd been there for a while, before Warren's arrival.

"Let me go with you," Warren offered. "In case you need backup."

Raleigh wasn't sure he wanted that, but he also didn't want to sit around here while his mom was in danger. Nor did he want to leave Warren out here by himself. He unlocked the back door of the cruiser and motioned for Warren to get in. The moment he did that, Raleigh sped toward the house.

He didn't see anyone else along the way, but there was a truck in front of the house that belonged to one of the ranch hands who was supposed to be keeping watch. He pulled the cruiser to a stop next to it. And cursed. Because the driver's-side door was open, but the ranch hand wasn't inside.

Raleigh hated to think the worst, but with

all the other attacks, it was the first possibility that came to mind. If someone had wanted to break into the house, they could have eliminated the ranch hands.

Since the driveway was on the side of the house and went all the way to the back, Raleigh kept driving. Kept looking. No one. But even from outside, he could hear the blare of the security system.

He pulled to a stop directly next to the back porch. "Wait here," Raleigh told Warren. "And let us know if anyone tries to come up behind us. Thea and I will go in and check on things." Maybe, just maybe, there'd be nothing wrong.

Raleigh glanced at Thea to make sure she was ready. She was. She had a firm grip on her gun as she opened the cruiser door. Raleigh did the same, but before he could even step out, he heard a hissing sound.

That was the only warning he got before the flames shot up in front of him.

THEA AUTOMATICALLY JUMPED back from the flames and put her hand in front of her face to shield it. But she was on full alert, too, because she knew that this could be some kind of diversion so that gunmen could kill them.

However, it also confirmed that this wasn't just a false alarm.

The threat was real, and that meant not only were they in danger but so were Alma and Alice.

Raleigh ran to her and pulled her back even farther. Like her, he shot glances all around them. So did Warren when he got out of the cruiser.

"The fire isn't touching the house," Raleigh let them know.

At least it wasn't yet. It appeared that someone had poured a line of accelerant and had lit it with perhaps a remote control. But if the breeze blew the flames into the house, it could catch the place on fire.

The fire was creating another problem, too. The smoke. It was thick and dark, and it seemed to come right at them, causing them all to cough. Worse, it was burning her eyes and making it hard to see. Definitely what she didn't want since someone could be out there.

Someone with plans to kill them.

Thea had figured there'd be another attack, but she'd thought it would come down to Raleigh and her against the person responsible for so much chaos. But now Warren was here, and that meant he was in danger, too. Maybe that had been part of the plan all along though.

"Cover me," Raleigh told Thea.

He headed to the far back right corner of the house, where there was some kind of control box. For the automatic sprinkler system, she soon realized. Raleigh hit the button to turn on all the nozzles, and they immediately began to pop up and start spraying water. It meant the three of them were getting wet, but it might keep the flames under control.

"I'll call the fire department," Warren offered, taking out his phone.

Good. And Dalton was on the way, too, but Thea didn't intend to wait. Especially not wait out in the open. With Raleigh ahead of her and Warren right behind, they started up the porch steps.

And they immediately stopped.

"Those are the two ranch hands who were supposed to be keeping watch," Raleigh whispered.

Oh, God. This wasn't good. Because she soon spotted the two men sprawled out on the porch.

"Are they dead?" she asked, afraid to hear the answer.

While Thea and Warren kept watch, Raleigh touched his fingers to one of the men's necks and then the other. "They're alive. It looks as if someone used a stun gun on them. Maybe drugged them, too."

The relief came, but it didn't last because someone had obviously gotten close enough to the hands to incapacitate them. And that someone could now be inside, doing the same, or worse, to Raleigh's mother and his deputy.

"I'll call for an ambulance," Warren volunteered.

Maybe the men wouldn't need medical attention right away, because an ambulance wouldn't be able to get onto the ranch until they were sure there wasn't a shooter nearby.

Raleigh went to the door. "Locked," he said, and he fished through his pocket for the keys.

Maybe the person who'd attacked the hands hadn't gone in through the back, but if he had, he'd clearly locked it behind him. Maybe to slow them down.

Or ambush them when they went in.

Once he had the door unlocked, Raleigh used the barrel of his gun to ease it open a couple of inches. Thea steeled herself up for some kind of attack.

But nothing happened.

Raleigh reached inside to the keypad, hit some buttons and the alarm stopped. Thea immediately tried to listen for any sounds coming from inside, but she heard nothing.

"According to the light on the security panel, the alarm was tripped with this door," Raleigh explained, his voice barely louder than a whisper.

So whoever had broken in had locked the door behind him. There were no obvious signs of forced entry, but someone skilled at picking a lock would be able to get in without leaving any obvious damage. Certainly though, an intruder would have guessed there'd be a security system. But maybe he didn't care, especially since the alarm would have masked his movements in the house.

But there was another possibility.

One that Thea hoped was what had actually happened. That the alarm had scared the guy off, and that he'd gone running. She wanted to confront this monster and stop him—or her—but she didn't want that to happen with Raleigh's mother or Warren around.

"Text Alice and tell her we're here and about to come in," Raleigh told her. "Ask her if they're okay."

Since Thea still had his phone, she did that and got a quick response back from Alice that Thea relayed to Raleigh. "They're fine. No one's tried to get into the room where they are."

Maybe it would stay that way.

Raleigh stepped into the kitchen. He didn't

turn on the lights and looked around before he motioned for Warren and her to join him. No smoke inside, thank goodness, but if the sprinkler didn't put out the flames, there soon would be. That meant they'd need to evacuate Alma and Alice. They didn't have a choice about that, but it came with huge risks since it meant they'd be outside, where they could be gunned down.

Raleigh's phone dinged with a message. At first, Thea thought it was Alice again, but it was Dalton this time.

When Thea read the text, her stomach clenched. "Someone put a spike strip on the road after we drove through. Dalton hit it and all the tires on his cruiser are flat. He'll have to wait for Miguel to come and give him a ride out here."

Raleigh mumbled some profanity. Whoever was behind this had wanted to make sure Dalton didn't arrive to help them. And it had worked. But what did this monster have planned for them?

"Tell Dalton not to come on foot," Raleigh instructed. "I don't want someone gunning him down."

Neither did she. Enough people had been hurt or killed.

"After Miguel picks him up," Raleigh went on, "Dalton and he can secure the perimeter of the house and get the two hands into the cruiser."

Thea sent the response to the deputy and then lifted her head to try to detect any trace of accelerant in the house. She didn't want a new fire trapping them inside, but there were no unusual smells. No unusual sounds, either.

Since this was the first time she'd been in Alma's house, she had no idea where the bedroom was, but Raleigh started out of the kitchen. But first he motioned for Warren to keep watch behind them. Thea made sure no one was on the sides of them. Hard to do though because the house was dark.

Raleigh led them through a family room and then a foyer. He tested the knob on the front door. "It's still locked," he whispered to them.

That was good because hopefully it meant no one could get in that way while they were walking up to the second floor. Raleigh went up the first three steps of the curved staircase and looked up, no doubt hoping to get a glimpse of whoever had broken in.

Thea certainly didn't see anything, but she heard something. Not a sound from the second floor or stairs, either. This had come from the living room on the other side of the foyer. Warren and Raleigh must have heard it, too, because they pivoted in that direction.

Just as someone fired a shot right at them.

Chapter Fourteen

"Get down!" Raleigh shouted.

And he prayed Thea and Warren could do that before they got shot.

Warren didn't get down though. He fired in the direction of the shooter.

Even though Raleigh couldn't see the gunman and Warren probably couldn't, either, the shot paid off because their attacker didn't pull the trigger again. Raleigh did hear him scrambling for cover in the living room though. That was good because it gave the three of them a chance to get off the stairs and out of the foyer and into the living room.

It wasn't ideal, but at least there was a partial wall they could use that might prevent them from being gunned down.

From the moment that Thea and he arrived at the ranch, Raleigh had been steeling himself up for an attack. An attack that he had hoped to prevent, but obviously it was too late for that.

But who was behind this?

Raleigh silently cursed that it was something he still didn't know. And he might not find it out anytime soon. Because the person who'd shot at them could be just another hired gun, someone doing the dirty work for Simon, Nick or Yvette.

Another shot came, and it slammed into the half wall. Since a bullet could easily go through it, Raleigh motioned for Thea and Warren to get to the side of the sofa. That would serve two purposes. Not only would it put some distance between the shooter and them, it would give them a better vantage point to make sure someone didn't sneak up on them by coming through the kitchen. The ranch hands were on the back porch, but even if they had regained consciousness, they still might not be able to stop someone else from getting inside.

His phone dinged just as there was another shot, and this bullet did rip through the drywall and went God knew where in the living room. Raleigh glanced back to make sure Thea and Warren were okay. They were. For now. But he motioned for them to get down.

"Alice texted," Thea whispered. "She heard the shots."

Of course she had. They were deafening, so that meant his mother had heard them, too, and she was probably terrified. Raleigh was feeling some fear of his own because he had to consider that this thug downstairs was just a distraction so his partner could get to Alma.

But if Alma was the target, why hadn't the person just bashed down the bedroom door after he'd broken in?

Why wait?

He couldn't think of a good reason for doing that. So that meant Thea, he or Warren was the target. Or maybe all three. But hopefully his mom would be out of harm's way while he figured out how to safely get to her.

Raleigh scrambled closer to Thea so the gunman wouldn't hear what he wanted her to text Alice. "Tell her that I want Mom and her in the bathtub."

That way, if this clown started shooting at the ceiling, Alice and his mother wouldn't get hit with stray shots.

While Thea sent off the message, Raleigh moved again so he could maybe catch of glimpse of the shooter. He hurried to the other side of the sofa, where he still had some cover, but he was also in a better position to take this guy out.

When the gunman leaned out to fire, Raleigh sent two bullets right at him. He couldn't tell though if he hit him, but at least it stopped the gunfire. Raleigh doubted that would last though.

And it didn't.

It only took a few seconds before the man leaned out again. This time, Raleigh didn't miss. His shot slammed into the guy, and he made a loud groan of pain before he collapsed onto the floor.

While he watched to make sure no one was at the top of the stairs, ready to shoot him, Raleigh went to the thug. The guy had on a ski mask, but Raleigh pulled it off him and checked for a pulse. Nothing.

"He's dead," Raleigh told the others. He made a quick study of the dead man's face, but didn't recognize him.

"You smell that?" Thea asked.

Raleigh was so focused on the shooter that it took him a moment to realize what she meant. *Smoke.*

And it didn't seem to be coming from outside.

"Stay put," Warren told Thea.

Before Raleigh could figure out if it was a good idea or not, Warren ran back toward the kitchen. Thea clearly didn't like that any better than Raleigh did, but they needed to know what was going on. And what was going on wasn't good. Raleigh could tell that from Warren's stark expression when he came back into the living room.

"Someone set a fire in the pantry." Warren's words rushed out with his frantic breath. "You have to get Alma and your deputy out of the house. And I need to move those hands off the porch in case the fire spreads back there."

Yes, he did. But that left Raleigh with a huge problem. He didn't want Warren on the porch without backup, especially when the man was trying to move the unconscious hands. But Raleigh didn't think it was a good idea for Thea to be outside, either. Still, that might be better than her being inside a house that was now on fire.

"Go with him," Raleigh told her.

She didn't argue, but he could practically feel the hesitation before she nodded. She tossed him his phone and followed Warren to the back.

Raleigh hated that it had come down to this. Yes, it was her job as a cop, but that didn't make this easier to swallow. He was afraid for Thea. Afraid he might never see her again.

And angry with himself for not telling her just how much she meant to him.

He pushed those feelings aside so he could go up the stairs and rescue his mother, but his phone dinged after he'd made it only a few steps. It was another text from Alice.

Someone's breaking into the bedroom.

Hell. For just a few words, they packed a wallop, and Raleigh practically ran up the stairs. Of course, he had to stop when he got to the top because whoever was trying to break into his mother's room would see him the moment he was in the hall.

Unfortunately, there were no lights on in the hall, so it took Raleigh a moment to pick through the darkness and see the shadowy figure outside the bedroom. And it appeared he was trying to get the door unlocked. Raleigh didn't shoot the guy because he couldn't even tell if he was armed.

"I'm Sheriff Lawton," Raleigh called out. "Put your hands in the air."

The man pivoted, and that's when Raleigh caught a glimpse of his gun. A gun he pointed at Raleigh. He didn't give the thug a chance to fire though because Raleigh pulled the trigger first. Two shots slammed into the man's chest, causing him to drop just as fast as his partner had minutes earlier.

Raleigh hurried to him. The guy was dead all right. That felt like a hard rock in his stomach, but he hadn't had another option. He couldn't let the guy shoot him. Nor could he let him break into the bedroom.

"Alice, it's me," Raleigh called out, knocking on the door. While he waited, he sent off a quick text to Thea to let her know he was okay. "There's a fire," he added to Alice, "and both of you need to get out of the house."

Almost immediately, he heard the sound of running footsteps, and a moment later, Alice opened the door. Alma was right behind her, and while his mom did indeed look terrified, he couldn't take the time to console her. The smoke was already making its way up the stairs, and he didn't want them trapped.

Alice hooked her arm around Alma's waist to get her moving, and both women glanced at the dead guy in the hall. Alma looked away, a hoarse sob coming from her throat.

"My house is on fire?" Alma asked. She was clearly alarmed by not just the dead man but also the fact that she might lose everything. Too bad that everything might include her life if there were other hired guns waiting outside.

"The fire department's on the way," Raleigh said.

Later, once he had everyone safe, he would

make sure that was true and fill her in on everything else that'd happened. Of course, the fire department was almost certainly nearby, or soon would be, but they were no doubt waiting on word from him to make sure it was safe to come onto the grounds. Right now, it definitely wasn't safe.

"Keep watch behind us," Raleigh told Alice just in case someone was hiding in another one of the bedrooms off the hall.

With Raleigh ahead of them, he led them to the stairs, hurrying as much as he could. But he also had to watch and listen to make certain they weren't about to be ambushed. He didn't see anyone at the bottom of the stairs or in the foyer, but that didn't mean someone wasn't there.

"The cruiser's parked right outside," he told Alice. "Get Mom inside, and I'll find the others." Including those two hands who could be hurt.

Opening the door was a risk, but everything he did at this point would be. Still, the cruiser was the safest place for his mother.

He eased open the door and looked out. No one. So Raleigh unlocked the cruiser and then handed the keys to Alice.

"You're not coming with us?" Alma asked. Her voice and the rest of her were shaking.

"I'll be there soon," he told her and hoped that was true. "Move fast," he added to Alice in a whisper. "And if something goes wrong, drive out of here as quickly as you can."

Alice nodded, and Raleigh stepped out onto the porch to give them cover as they ran to the cruiser. However, Alice and his mom hadn't even gotten in yet when he heard something that caused his heart to slam against his chest.

"No!" someone shouted, and Raleigh was

pretty sure that someone was Warren, who was at the back of the house.

And the shout was followed by another sound Raleigh didn't want to hear.

A gunshot.

THEA TRIED TO keep watch of the backyard as she pulled one of the hands off the porch and away from the fire. It wasn't easy. He was a big guy, and since she couldn't lift him, she had no choice but to drag him down the steps and toward the grassy area behind the house.

Warren was doing the same thing to the second hand, and he was struggling as much as Thea was. She only hoped this wasn't doing more damage to Warren's already injured body, but even if it had, it wouldn't have stopped him.

The sprinklers didn't help the situation, either. They were still going full blast, and while that appeared to be containing the fire in the yard, it was also soaking Warren and her. Plus, the combination of water and smoke in her eyes made it even harder to see.

She'd just made it to the bottom step when she heard the two shots from inside the house. It caused her pulse to skyrocket because they had almost certainly come from the second floor, where Raleigh would be rescuing his mom and Alice.

Thea looked up at the windows but couldn't see anything, and she forced herself not to run inside. However, the second her phone dinged with a text message, she stopped dragging the ranch hand and looked at the screen. It was from Raleigh. We're okay.

The breath of relief rushed out of her, and she prayed it was true, that Raleigh hadn't told her that just to stop her from going inside. She would though. As soon as she'd finished moving the hand, she needed to make sure Raleigh, Alice and his mom had made it out. That meant going inside.

Thea kept dragging the hand. She had to get the man far enough away from the house in case the fire caused it to collapse. He still hadn't regained consciousness, and there was no way he'd be able to move to save himself.

"Over here," Warren told her.

He motioned toward the front of a small barn, where he was heading. It wasn't ideal cover because both ends were wide-open, but it would give them some protection from the sides. As it was now, they were out in the open, where anyone could gun them down.

"Was Raleigh hurt?" Warren asked, and he didn't sound like a lawman but rather a concerned father.

She shook her head. "He said they were all okay."

Thea's arms were aching by the time she

reached the barn, but she got the hand in. It was like stepping into a cave since it was so dark. Too dark for her to see any of the corners. Plus, there was a tractor and some other equipment, plenty of places for someone to hide. That's why she took a moment to listen and made sure no one was inside. If someone was, he or she wasn't making a sound.

Since Warren was struggling, she went out to help him drag in the second hand, and she positioned him next to the other one.

"Wait here with them in case the fire comes this way and they need to be moved again," she told Warren. She tried to wipe some of the water off her face. "I need to check on Raleigh to see if he needs any help getting Alma out."

She expected Warren to argue with that because he didn't like her going out there without backup. And he no doubt wanted to argue, but he probably knew it wouldn't do any good. Instead, he huffed.

"Don't go in through the back," he warned her.

She wouldn't. By now, the fire had probably spread into the kitchen. Or maybe even farther into the house. That meant she'd need to go on the side so she could get to the front porch. But hopefully that's where Raleigh would be if he had indeed managed to get his mom and Alice out of the house.

Before she could start running, Warren caught on to her hand and made eye contact with her. It was so dark that it was hard to fully see his expression, but his forehead was bunched up with worry.

"Be careful," he said.

She was about to remind him to do the same thing, but then she saw the change in Warren's body language. His shoulders went back, and he started lifting his gun.

"No!" Warren shouted, his attention on the area behind her.

That was the only warning Thea got before the gunshot blasted through the air.

For a horrifying moment, she thought Warren or she had been shot. But the bullet went into the barn just as Warren grabbed hold of her and yanked her to the floor.

At least that's what he tried to do.

But someone took hold of her from behind, hooking his arm around her throat. In the same motion, he knocked her Glock from her hand and put a gun to her head.

The fear and adrenaline slammed into her, and her body went into fight mode. She rammed her elbow into his stomach, but it didn't work. The man was wearing some kind of body armor, and he didn't loosen his grip. In fact, he tightened it and dug the barrel of the gun into her temple.

Warren cursed and froze, his weapon aimed

at an attacker she couldn't see, but he must have realized he didn't have a shot, because Warren scrambled to the side of the tractor. Good. At least he wouldn't be gunned down—which was probably what her attacker had planned to do because he fired another bullet in Warren's direction.

"Let go of her," Warren demanded.

Thea doubted that would work, and it didn't. The man held on. But he didn't start to move as if to escape, and he didn't fire any other shots at Warren. He seemed to be waiting for something. But what did he want and why was he doing this?

"Not much longer now," he growled in her ear. His voice was a raspy whisper. Maybe it was Nick or Simon, but it could be just another hired thug. One that maybe Yvette had sent to attack them.

When she heard someone running toward them, the man shifted her body so that she was facing the opening of the barn. He stayed behind her, using her as a shield.

Just as Raleigh came into view.

He'd obviously run through the sprinklers because he was wet, and even though he had his gun aimed and ready, he didn't have a clean shot. However, he must have been able to see her attacker's face because Raleigh cursed.

"What the hell do you think you're doing?" Raleigh snapped.

"Finishing this," the man readily answered. He didn't whisper this time though, and Thea had no trouble recognizing his voice.

It was Simon.

A DOZEN THOUGHTS went through Raleigh's head, and none of them were good.

First and foremost though was that Thea was in grave danger. He could lose her right here, right now, to this sick piece of work. Raleigh had to stay alive to try to save her, and that's why he took cover by the side of the barn door.

Thea had to be terrified, but she was clearly trying to rein in her fear. Warren wasn't even attempting the facade. Raleigh could practically feel Warren's rage, and he shook his head, hoping it would keep Warren from launching himself at Simon. Raleigh wanted to try to defuse this, and that wouldn't happen if gunfire broke out.

And it wasn't just Thea and Warren he had to be concerned about. The two hands were on the barn floor, and they could easily be hit with gunfire. Simon basically had five people's lives in his hands.

"I thought you were in love with my mother," Raleigh reminded Simon. He kept watch around them, trying to make sure Simon didn't have another goon who would try to sneak up on them. "You've got a funny way of showing it since you nearly killed her with the fire you had your hired thug set. And now her house is burning down."

No way for Raleigh to save the house. Because it was too risky for him to get the fire department on the grounds. Hopefully Alice had managed to get his mother far from here.

"I *was* in love with Alma," Simon snapped. "Until I read that letter about her still having feelings for Warren. I've waited in the wings for years for her to be through with him, and just when I finally thought it had happened, Alma does something like this."

So that letter was the motive, and Raleigh could fill in the rest. "You killed Sonya and Hannah to get back at Warren, to punish him."

"And it worked. Warren nearly went crazy blaming himself and trying to figure out who killed Hannah." Simon smiled, but it quickly faded. "Except Sonya wasn't supposed to die. The men were supposed to kidnap her, but they overreacted when she escaped and ran."

"They murdered her," Raleigh pointed out. "Since you hired them, you're guilty of murder, too. And endangering the babies. How the hell could you do something like that to them?"

"I didn't endanger them, and I sure as heck didn't hurt them," Simon yelled. He glanced around, too, as if looking for something. Or someone. "Hannah's baby was well cared for, and Thea would have already been dead, but she was too close to Sonya's kid, so Marco couldn't shoot her."

That's why Thea had been spared. All because she was in the wrong place at the wrong time. Another minute before or after, and the baby might not have been close enough to her, and Marco or Buck would have gunned her down. Like Simon was planning to do.

Or not.

Simon obviously had already had a chance to kill her, so why hadn't he? Was he waiting for Warren to come out from cover so he could shoot him first?

Or did Simon plan to kill both Thea and him in front of Warren?

That way, Warren would lose his son and the woman he loved like a daughter. If that was what Simon had in mind, then Raleigh had to stop him. That meant buying himself some time so he could figure out how to safely launch himself at Simon.

"Why involve Sonya, Hannah and Thea in this? Why didn't you just kill me?" Warren growled.

Simon's mouth tightened into a sneer. "Because I loved Alma enough that I didn't want her to grieve. I wanted her over and done with you, and if you'd been murdered, you would have become a martyr to her. That's why I didn't rat you out to your wife and kids. To Raleigh," he added.

Maybe. But Simon might have been worried that Warren would have chosen Alma instead of his wife and family. That definitely wouldn't have worked in Simon's favor to try to win Alma's heart.

"Everything I've done has been for Alma," Simon insisted. "That should prove to you how much I loved her."

No, it only proved that Simon was pathetic. And a killer.

A killer who clearly planned to murder Thea, but he wasn't trying to do that. Why? Simon had Warren right where he wanted him.

A moment later, Raleigh had his answer to that, and it wasn't an answer he liked.

"Finally," Simon snapped.

Raleigh heard the movement behind him, and he turned in that direction. And his heart skipped a couple of beats. Because there was a ski-mask-wearing thug coming toward him, and he wasn't alone.

He had Alma with him.

Hell. This was the reason Simon hadn't already added more murders to his list of crimes. He wanted to kill Alma in front of Warren. Or vice versa. Either way, Simon would almost certainly then try to murder all of them since he couldn't leave this many witnesses alive.

"Where's Alice?" Raleigh asked.

"This jerk used a stun gun on her," Alma answered, her voice cracking. "We didn't see him in time. Before Alice could drive away, he pulled her from the cruiser and left her on the driveway when he took me. Raleigh, I'm so sorry."

He hated that his mom felt the need to apologize for a thug assaulting a deputy and then manhandling her. Hated even more that this was happening. One way or another though, he would stop it. He just had to make sure he didn't get anyone killed in the process.

"Simon," his mother said, her voice quivering even more. She shifted her attention to Thea, then Raleigh and finally Warren. With each shift, her eyes got wider, and he could see the horror on her face when she realized what was happening. "Simon," she repeated.

"Don't look at me like that," Simon growled at her. "You're responsible for this."

"He read the letter," Raleigh told her.

Alma shook her head. "And you felt you had to do this because I still love Warren?" She didn't wait for an answer. "Because Warren doesn't love me. He's back with his wife, and it's over between us."

The glare that Simon gave Alma was scalpel sharp. "It'll never be over between you. Never. But it ends now. Everything ends."

Simon tipped his head to the masked thug, and the man shoved Alma forward, right into Raleigh. Raleigh didn't catch her because it would have meant taking his aim off Simon, but he used his body to help break the fall, and then he maneuvered himself in front of her.

Raleigh braced himself for Simon and his hired gun to start shooting, but the thug took off running. He ran past them and to the back opening of the barn, where Raleigh saw him press something he took from his pocket. Moments later, there was a hissing sound, and the flames shot up in front of the barn.

Alma screamed, and Raleigh prayed it wasn't because the fire had burned her. Even if it had, he couldn't take the time to check because he had to get her out of there. Not in the direction of the fire, either. Raleigh dragged her into the barn.

"If any of you move, Thea will be the first to die," Simon warned them.

Raleigh looked at Simon's face, and that's when he knew. Simon intended for all of them to die.

Warren moved closer to the end of the tractor. No doubt so he'd be in a better position to return fire if he got the chance. Right now, neither Warren nor he had a clean shot, so he had to do something to tip the odds in their favor.

"Get down," Raleigh whispered to his mom, and he hoped she listened. If not, Simon might try to shoot her.

Warren came out from behind the tractor, causing Simon to turn his gun in his direction. Thea took full advantage of no longer having the barrel pressed to her head. She shoved her weight against Simon, causing him to become off-balanced just enough so that when he pulled the trigger, his shot missed.

Simon fired again.

And again.

Thea scrambled away from Simon, making a beeline to her gun that was on the floor. But before she could even reach it, the shot rang out.

It seemed as if time had frozen. Raleigh thought maybe his heart had, too. He knew he hadn't been the one to pull the trigger, but obviously someone had.

This time, it wasn't Simon.

Raleigh saw the shock register on the man's face. Then saw the blood spread across the front of his shirt. Clutching his chest, Simon dropped to his knees, his stare frozen on the person who'd just put a bullet in him.

Alma.

His mother had snatched up Thea's gun. And she hadn't missed. If the shot hadn't killed him, it soon would because he was bleeding out fast.

Despite what had played out in front of him, Raleigh quickly shifted his attention to the thug at the back of the barn. The man had already lifted his gun and was about to fire. But Raleigh fired first. The guy didn't fall on his knees but rather face-first onto the ground.

The adrenaline was still slamming hard through Raleigh, but he checked to make sure everyone was okay. He pulled Thea to her feet. No blood, thank God. It was the same for Warren. But when he looked back at his mother, the adrenaline spun right out of control.

Because his mother had been shot.

Chapter Fifteen

Everyone who mattered was alive. That's what Raleigh kept reminding himself as they sat in the ER waiting room. Thea, his deputies, the drugged ranch hands and yes, even Warren had made it through the hellish nightmare. But at the moment, it didn't feel like a victory.

Because his mother might not make it.

That wasn't easy for him to consider. Especially since the man who'd put the bullet in her had been her friend for as long as Raleigh could remember. At least the *friend* was now dead, and so were all the thugs he'd hired to

368 Under the Cowboy's Protection

carry out his sick plan of revenge against Warren and Alma.

Thea was seated next to Raleigh, resting her head against his shoulder. Her hair and clothes were still damp from the soaking they'd gotten with the sprinklers, and she smelled like smoke. No physical injuries, but she had that stark look in her eyes. The one that told Raleigh that what'd happened this night would stay with her forever. It might be something she could never get past. And since he was part of those nightmarish memories, too, Thea might be done with him, as well.

Warren wasn't faring much better. He was sitting across from Thea and him. Again, no injuries, but he had his head in his hands, and every now and then he made a soft groaning sound. He definitely looked as if he needed some rest. And maybe some pain meds since Raleigh knew Warren was still recovering from his own shooting that'd happened a while back.

"If you want to go on home to your wife and kids," Raleigh told him, "I'll call you with any updates."

Raleigh immediately wished he hadn't worded it like that. It sounded bitter. Which he wasn't. Well, not bitter about Warren anyway. It was going to take a while before he didn't feel such things about Simon.

"Helen knows I'm here," Warren said.

Helen was his wife, and Raleigh knew Warren had called both his son Egan and her shortly after they'd arrived at the hospital. Raleigh had only heard bits and pieces of Warren's side of the conversation, but he'd told them that he was fine and there was no reason for them to come and get him. Whether or not they would stay away was anyone's guess.

"Helen is okay with you being here?" Thea asked.

There was plenty of hesitation in her voice. But it was a good question. Raleigh wanted to know the same thing. Warren had put enough strain on his marriage without adding more. Just his being here could be *more* in Helen's eyes.

Warren took his time answering. "Helen's worried about me, but she knows why I need to be here. Because of Thea and you."

There it was again. The confusion swirled with all the other things Raleigh was feeling.

"I know," Warren added a moment later. He no doubt saw the mixed emotions on Raleigh's face. "You don't want me to worry about you, but you're my son, and worry comes with the territory of being a father. And for the record, I worried about you even before my relationship with your mother came to light. I know I wasn't involved in your life, but I loved you," he said in a mumble.

Raleigh wasn't sure he wanted to hear that love thing. But at least it didn't twist at him the way it usually did when he thought about Warren being his father. Maybe that was a start. Thea must have thought so because she managed a very short, very slight smile.

The silence settled among them for several long moments before Warren shook his head again. "I should have figured out it was Simon and should have stopped him before it came down to this."

Raleigh gave a frustrated sigh because he felt the same way.

Thea, however, huffed, and this time when she lifted her head from Raleigh's shoulder, there was no trace of a smile. "I could have missed it in the job description, but a badge or a former badge doesn't give you ESP. Simon hid his true self from a lot of people, and he's the only person to blame for what happened. The. Only. Person," she emphasized.

Raleigh looked at her, their eyes connecting, and he was relieved to see that what she'd said wasn't lip service. That was big of her since he'd come damn close to letting her die tonight.

At least the babies hadn't been around for this particular attack, and now that Simon and his hired guns were dead, they were out of danger. Soon, Hannah's baby would be reunited with her birth parents—something they were eager for. Sonya's daughter might be a little trickier. According to the last call Raleigh had gotten from Miguel, they would still need the DNA results before handing over the child that Hannah had delivered.

Raleigh's phone dinged, indicating he had another text message. He'd gotten a lot of them in the hour that they'd been at the hospital since his mom's ranch was now a crime scene that had to be processed. Or at least it would be once the fire department and medical examiner cleared out and took the bodies to the morgue.

"It's from Miguel," Raleigh told Thea when she glanced at his phone. It wasn't the best of news, but it was what he'd expected. "They managed to put out the fire, but most of Mom's house was destroyed."

"Alma's stronger than she looks. She'll get through this and will rebuild," Warren said, and then his forehead bunched up when he glanced at Raleigh. "Sorry."

Raleigh wasn't sure exactly what the apology was for. Maybe because Warren didn't want to remind him that he knew enough about Alma to make comments like that. But it was the truth. His mom was strong, especially under pressure.

First though, she had to stay alive.

"If it's all right, I'd like to be the one to call Hannah's kin," Warren continued a moment later, and he was talking to Raleigh. "I want to tell them who was responsible for her death. It won't be much comfort to them because it won't bring her back, but at least they'll know."

Raleigh nodded, and it was a reminder that he needed to tell Sonya's relatives, as well.

"So, what will happen with you two?" Warren asked.

The question threw Raleigh, and it caused Thea to pull back her shoulders. She looked at him. Raleigh looked at her. And he realized he didn't have a clue what the answer was. But he knew what he wanted to happen.

He wanted to put the past behind them and be with Thea.

Raleigh wasn't even sure that was possible though.

He didn't get a chance to start figuring it out, either, because he saw Dr. Jacobs, the surgeon, making his way toward them. Thea, Warren and he all stood, and Raleigh could tell they were doing what he was—trying to steel himself up for whatever the news might be.

"Alma made it through surgery just fine," Dr. Jacobs immediately said.

Raleigh hadn't expected the relief to hit him so hard, but it nearly knocked the breath out of him. It did the same to Thea because she practically sagged against him. He looped his arm around her waist in case her legs felt as unsteady as his did.

"The bullet didn't hit anything vital, and I

was able to remove it with only a small incision," the doctor went on. "She'll have to stay in the hospital a couple of days, of course, but I expect her to make a full recovery."

"When can I see her?" Raleigh asked.

"You can pop into recovery for just a second or two. She's woozy but awake. Follow me," the doctor instructed. Dr. Jacobs started to move but then stopped and looked at Thea and Warren. "I can only allow immediate family in the recovery room, but if you're close to Alma, you'll be able to see her from the observation window."

Warren shook his head. "I'll just be going. I need to get home." He hugged Thea. "I'm not offering you a ride," he added to her, and even though Warren had whispered it, Raleigh still heard it. "Stay here and work things out with Raleigh."

That sounded like approval for a relationship between Thea and him. Not that Raleigh needed approval from Warren. But it still felt good to get it.

Warren stepped back from Thea and extended his hand to Raleigh. Again, it wasn't much, just a small gesture, but it felt like they were moving in the right direction. Raleigh shook his hand, and judging from the way Warren smiled, it seemed as if Raleigh had handed him the moon. Warren tipped his hat to Dr. Jacobs and headed out while Thea and he followed the doctor down the hall.

"Your mother might not be so happy to see me," Thea muttered, suddenly sounding uncomfortable.

"She's alive. We're alive. That'll make her happy."

Raleigh meant that, too, but he wasn't sure what he'd see when they approached the recovery room. His mother had just been shot.

And had killed a man. She might not bounce back from that anytime soon.

Thea stopped at the window while Raleigh went in, but Alma lifted her hand and motioned for Thea to join him.

"Immediate family only," the doctor reminded Alma.

"Thea's practically family," Alma insisted. "Or she should be."

Coming on the heels of Warren's *So, what will happen with you two* question, this felt like matchmaking. Badly timed matchmaking at that. Thea might still be in shock, and he didn't want to press her with Warren's question or anything else.

Thea walked into the room, her steps slow and cautious. "How are you feeling?" she asked his mother.

His mother managed to eke out a smile, though it was clear she was weak and sleepy from the drugs. "Better now that you two are here." The smile didn't last though, and there were tears in her eyes when she looked at Raleigh. "I had to kill Simon. If I hadn't—"

"None of us would be here," Raleigh interrupted. "You saved our lives. Warren's, too." He debated if he should add more about that, but his mother appeared to be waiting for him to continue. "He stayed here until he found out you were out of the woods, and then he went home."

No need to add that he was going home to his wife. Alma knew that. And she nodded. "Good." And it seemed genuine.

Love had definitely given her a kick in the teeth, but maybe one day she could put aside her feelings for Warren and find someone who didn't make her part of his secrets and lies. Of course, without those secrets and lies, Raleigh wouldn't exist.

"The house is gone, I suppose?" Alma asked.

He hadn't planned to bring it up, but since she had, Raleigh nodded. "I'll do the insurance paperwork to get the rebuild started, and you can stay with me until it's done."

"Thea won't mind if I'm there?" his mother pressed.

"Of course not," Thea jumped to answer. "There's no reason for me to mind." In fact, she said it so fast that it made Raleigh wonder if Thea had plans to avoid his place altogether.

Alma took Thea by the hand and inched her closer to the bed. "You'll always be close to Warren. I would never want to change that. I just want you to know that I'll welcome you, too. I mean, it's as plain as the nose on my face that you're in love with my son."

Thea pulled in her breath, and Raleigh thought some of the color drained from her face. She didn't get a chance to respond though because the doctor tapped his watch. "Your time's up. You can visit Alma in the morning, after we've moved her out of recovery."

Raleigh nodded and then brushed a kiss on his mom's cheek. "Get some rest."

"Tell her you love her," his mom countered, and she quickly closed her eyes, no doubt a ploy so he wouldn't argue with her.

Yeah, she was definitely matchmaking.

Raleigh didn't say anything until they were out of the recovery room and back in the hall that led to the waiting area. "Sorry about what my mom said."

Thea stopped and looked at him. Actually, she glared a little. "I'm not sorry. If she hadn't brought it up, I would have. I'm in love with you." But she immediately continued without giving him a chance to respond. "It's okay if you don't feel the same way. No pressure. But

I'm tired of pretending that it's only an attraction between us. For me, it's a whole lot more."

Since it sounded as if she was getting a little angry—and because she wouldn't let him get a word in edgewise—he pulled her to him and kissed her. He made sure it was way too long and way too hot for a hospital hallway. But he'd wanted to make a point. Unfortunately, the point-making got a little clouded when Thea moved right into that kiss.

Thea and he kept it up until he heard someone clear their throat. A nurse, who was smiling at them but had her eyebrow raised. Raleigh knew her. She was Betsy Fay Millard, and she was a close friend of his mother's. Which meant Alma would soon know about this.

And would no doubt approve.

Betsy Fay hitched her thumb to the room next to them. "It's empty if you two need to work something out." She winked at them and strolled away.

Raleigh supposed he should be a little embarrassed about kissing Thea like that in a public place, but embarrassment wasn't a barrier to what he needed to get done. He took Thea into the room and kissed her again, all the while trying to figure out how to tell her the most important thing he'd ever have to tell her.

The second kiss lasted as long as he could make it last until they both needed air. And when they broke away from each other, Thea looked up at him and smiled. That was it. She didn't say anything. Didn't have to. Because he could see in her eyes every drop of the love she felt for him.

Man, it was amazing.

And just like that, everything suddenly felt right, as if all the pieces of his life had lined up the way they should. That made it a whole lot easier for him to say what was on his mind.

"I love you, Thea." Raleigh didn't have to think about it—he meant it with all his heart.

"Took you long enough," she joked. Some tears watered her eyes, but since she was smiling, he thought that was a good thing. She wadded up a handful of his shirt and pulled him back to her.

Raleigh made sure the third kiss was one they would both remember.

* * * * *